VORTEX

SACRIFICED BY

CURIOSITY

FOR LITERARY HEAT

WARNING: This book is for sale to **ADULT AUDIENCES ONLY**. Contains graphic gay male sex, reluctance, anal sex, non-graphic violence, BDSM, satanic practices, and gay love all of which may be considered offensive by some readers.

All sexually active characters in this work are at least 18 years of age.

BarbarianSpy
Toronto, NSW 2283
Australia

VORTEX:

SACRIFICED BY CURIOSITY

by

HABU

CONTENTS

CHAPTER ONE: CURIOSITY LEADS TO A NEW LIFESTYLE

Doug had been conditioning me for months. We had met at the gym, and several weeks after we'd become regular spotting partners, he revealed to me, almost in an off-hand manner, that he was bisexual and that he actually preferred gay sex. He didn't come on to me—at least not directly—and I consider myself fairly open-minded, so I continued with our informal spotting arrangements, him monitoring me as I worked the weights and me doing the same for him. I also had an insatiable curiosity, and Doug was quite clever about exploiting that curiosity. He wasn't the one who said or did anything about my trying out the gay lifestyle; he just responded to my natural curiosity. How was I to know, though, that this seemingly innocuous quirk was but the beginning of a long spiral down into the maelstrom?

Sometimes after we'd worked out and showered, we'd go someplace together for a drink before going our separate ways. As time went on, I started asking him about his life and about the whole gay scene. I don't know why I did this—or didn't know at the time. Looking at it in hindsight, he obviously had seen the curiosity in me for all sorts of things and had played on that from the beginning.

Regardless, the more he didn't push the topic, the more curious I was, the more I asked about it, and the more I became interested in it. After a while, he wasn't at all shy about watching me in the shower, but I guess I wasn't all that shy about watching him either. He slowly made his interest in me known in no uncertain terms. I remember going weak in the knees the first time I saw him hard in the shower. He must have had at least nine long, thick, hard inches jutting out from his balls. He was a good seven and a half inches just dangling. I hadn't been even vaguely interested in men in terms of sex before I'd met Doug, but now my curiosity was entertaining all sorts of "what ifs."

During that period, Doug didn't touch me with anything but his eyes, however, and the longer he went without trying to make a direct move on me, the more curious I became about his lifestyle and the more attractive he himself appeared to me. He had the blond good looks and robust, big-boned and heavily muscled physique that went with his Nordic heritage. His broad, open smile and ready humor also came straight from Scandinavia.

Whenever I was well into quizzing him about the gay lifestyle and why he was like he was, he would insert the hint that I might like to try it, and I'll confess that the more we talked and socialized with each other, the more curious I became about what he saw in this gay business that was better than a good fuck with a hot woman. I'd seen the way the women eyed him in the gym, so I knew that his lifestyle was definitely something he preferred and had chosen. I also saw how some of the men ogled him, and this only served to stoke my own curiosity. But still, no matter how closely we spiraled into trying it together, he never laid a hand on me in those early days other than to keep me from getting hurt from a falling weight during a gym workout.

That was until I fell from the rings one evening and he caught me by the crotch with one hand and his other hand slid up under my T-shirt and cupped one of my pecs. We stayed in that position perhaps for a second or two longer than was necessary, and he could hardly avoid noticing that my dick came alive under his touch. I could tell that he was impressed with what he'd felt by the look he gave me when we parted.

That evening, after our workout, while we were drinking beer in our usual bar, he finally moved in on his pitch. I don't remember how he maneuvered me into the proposition, but it was I who asked him if he'd do it with me just once so that I'd have some idea what his attraction to it was. By not making a direct move on me, he had caused me to start to doubt my own attraction and wondering if someone like him just didn't want someone like me. But, when I brought it up, he came alive and put on that broad smile, and I knew that he had just wanted it to be me who made the proposal.

Strangely, though, we didn't just go off and do it then. He went to great lengths to ascertain that I'd never done it with a man before—that I hadn't been fucked before and hadn't so much as let another man touch my cock or balls.

This seemed a little odd to me; I assumed that all gay men fucked indiscriminately like rabbits, while wearing condoms when they did it, of course. But I did assure him that I was a virgin in the sense of any kind of sex with a man.

This declaration pleased Doug greatly, but again, strangely, he didn't suggest that we march off and get it on right there and then but suggested that I go with him to a private party the following week after our gym workout, where there would be a room we could use for all night if we wanted to. He pressed me for assurances that I really was interested in doing this, and I told him that the only reservation I had was that I had seen him hard, and I was scared about making nine inches disappear up my ass. He had smiled and said that I must really be terrified at the thought of twelve inches then, and we had both broken down into laughter.

I hadn't had any idea how much my curiosity had worked me up for this, but I walked around with a hard-on and a vision of those nine inches at Doug's midsection for most of the week in anticipation of having this experience with Doug. My butt twitched from the very thought of it, even though I was giving equal thought to the certain pain and possible pleasure of the experience.

On the night of the party, I trembled through our workout so badly that I couldn't manage to complete half my routine. Doug kept clucking and smiling at me and telling me that it would all go off just fine. He did hand me a small bottle and tell me to use it to take an enema and to shower really well before we went to the party, though, saying that good hygiene was a turn on and my virgin ass canal was going to get quite a workout. Not having the vaguest notion what men did to prepare to have sex with other men, I found this instruction alone so sexy that I almost creamed myself as Doug watched me shower.

We left my car in the gym parking lot and took Doug's. It was a dark night, and he soon had me lost in a maze of unlit streets in a far suburban section of town I'd never been in. At length, we turned into a drive and up to a set of large gates that opened to a clicker Doug pulled out of a compartment in his dashboard, and we slowly swept up to and parked on the grass beside several other cars in front of a large Georgian mansion.

The party was men only, as I had anticipated, and the entertainment rooms were heavy with smoke, not all of it from cigarettes, booze, testosterone, and the heavy musky smell of men in heat, on the edge of busting out in full rut. I don't know why, but this excited me and made me determined to drop all of my inhibitions, if at least for this evening. As Doug and I moved through the crowd, I cupped one of his butt cheeks in my hand, but he took my hand in his and moved it away from his body.

Uncertainty. He had told me that he was going to make love to me this evening, telling me in very detailed terms about his favorite sidesplitting position, and yet he still was avoiding intimacy.

He took me to a sofa toward the back of one of the many lounge-type rooms on the mansion's ground floor, somewhat away from the swirl of men around the floor, and we sat down. He did put his arm around me then.

But almost immediately after we sat down, my view of the room was cut off by the appearance of an older man, probably somewhere around forty but in very good shape, who came and stood directly in front of us. Doug introduced me to the man, who turned out to be the host of the party. I was told his name was Donatien. I raised an eyebrow at the fancy French name, but he just laughed and said I could call him Don. My first impression was that he must be a dancer. He was lithe but well muscled and moved with a smooth grace. He was dark and hirsute, with a close-cut mustache and beard that came to a point below his chin, heavy eyebrows twisted up at the ends, and long hair that came down below his shoulders. The most striking aspect of him was his eyes; they were violet and piercing. I felt that he could look right through me and discern my thoughts—or at least to completely undress me.

Don sat down beside me so that I was closely sandwiched between Doug and him. And, although Doug kept his arm behind my neck and his hand with a tight hold on my bicep, it was Don who started to make moves on me there on the sofa.

I had fully intended on having sex with Doug at this party, but this was something entirely new, something I hadn't bargained for or agreed to.

But Don was mesmerizing. He had his hand on my thigh, holding it in a firm grip with long, elegant fingers, and all the while he was telling me how beautiful Doug had said my body was and that he could see now that Doug hadn't been exaggerating. He mentioned that Doug told him we worked out together and his hand fluttered over my chest and down my abs and across my belly briefly as if he was checking out what Doug had told him, and then it went back, higher on my thigh. The hand went between my legs, and he pushed them apart, and I involuntarily found myself accommodating him and letting my legs spread. I had no idea what I was or was not supposed to be doing in this situation. I do remember having the sensation that I was some sort of race horse being auctioned off, though. I was entirely flustered and was angry at Doug for just sitting there, holding me in place for this assault, but not making any moves on me himself. I had come here for Doug's touch, not to be handed over as a party favor.

Don was turned to me now and had managed to get me to make eye contact with him, and I was lost in those violet eyes. As he murmured reassuring flattery to me, his hand went to my basket and traced my lengthening and thickening cock through the thin fabric of my pants and briefs.

I could feel Doug trembling beside me and wondered wildly why he wasn't doing anything. I could tell that he wanted me by the way his pants were tenting at his crotch. I moved my hand toward his basket, but he quickly grabbed it with his hand and held my hand immobile between us. My other arm was trapped behind Don's back. Between them, they had me pinned to this spot.

Don's hand snaked up under my shirt tail, and he tested and prodded my belly, abs, and pecs and squeezed my nipples gently. I began to breathe heavily and tried, in vain, to writhe away from his searching fingers. His hand slid down across my belly and continued under the waistband of my pants and found my dick and balls. Meanwhile, his other hand had slipped behind me and down my spine, and a long finger was snaking its way down below my waistband, between the crack of my butt cheeks, and rested very near to my asshole. I shuddered and gave a little moan.

He broke eye contact and his lips went to the side of my neck, where my carotid artery was pumping blood through my body at a rapid rate. I felt sharp teeth scrape against my vein, but he hesitated there just a few seconds. He gave me a sucky kiss there and then lifted his head and made eye contact with me again.

Staring deeply into my eyes, he started quizzing me in a low voice, just as Doug inexplicably had done a week before. Was I virgin to the touch of men? Never been touched by another man or touched another man before just now, let alone been kissed anywhere on the body, sucked off or given suck, or fucked? Was I quite sure?

My halting and bewildered answers seemed to satisfy him, and suddenly he had pulled his hands away from me and was reaching for the drink he had put on the floor next to the sofa before he sat down. He took a long swig from the drink, and then, turning to me, he held my face between his hands and forced my lips open with his and went into a long, deep kiss. His violet eyes held mine enthralled, as his tongue pushed deeper into my mouth.

But it wasn't just his tongue. He had transferred a couple of capsules to my mouth with his, and he was forcing them down my throat with his tongue. I gagged, but I swallowed them. There was nothing else I could do. They immediately started to have an effect on me. I was blacking out, as I had the sensation of both Don and Doug rising from the sofa and Doug hauling me over his shoulder like I was a sack of seed.

CHAPTER TWO: THE PARTY BEGINS; PREPARATION FOR RITUAL

When I awoke, still very groggy, I found I was completely naked, with my arms suspended from overhead hooks with chains and my legs spread apart and attached by chains to a stone floor as well. We were in some sort of stone vault. I had what seemed to be a wooden stool supporting me from behind and below so that I didn't drag my arms out of their sockets against the chains in my unconsciousness.

I felt wetness all over my body and became barely conscious that all of my body hair was being shaved off me with foam and straight razors, except for the hair on top of my head and my eyebrows. A man I barely remember from the crowd at the party was working on my right armpit and Doug, himself, was quite carefully shaving my pubic hair and my balls. Someone else was working on a thigh and a calf.

They were pretty much finished as I came at least partially out of my stupor and began to test my chains. Doug was washing me off—everywhere—with a wet, scented cloth. I found that all of my limbs had a bit of freedom of motion, but not much. The hooks of the chains attached to my arms and legs ran in groves along the floor and stone ceiling, and the grooves ran up into pillars in front of me and behind me, which indicated that the position of my body could be readily changed without freeing me. My wrists and ankles were heavily padded where they were cuffed to the chains. I had never felt so exposed and controlled before in my life.

I would have let everyone know how little I appreciated being trussed up like this, but I was still groggy and was completely awed by what I could see. About fifteen feet in front of me, in the middle of the room, was a low-slung altar, with a large brazier on top, which was emitting heavy, musk-scented smoke. But even more awesome were the men in the room. Although I recognized several as having been at the party in the mansion and the sexual allure had been heavy in the air there, the current context of their presence here was highly confusing and had entered an entirely new sexual dimension. They were swirling about the stone vault and all were naked to the waist. All wore tight, latex-like red leotards, open at both the crotch and the ass. They all were in superb shape, well-endowed to a man, even though of widely different body builds and types, and all had at least half hard-ons. They also all wore horns on their heads, which made them appear to be satyrs, which, no doubt, was what they were pretending to be. They were drinking heavily from flagons, and many were smoking joints or popping pills as they glided about the room, touching each other intimately in passing.

Then, out of the smoke, emerged a man who appeared to be the host of the party: Donatien. In contrast to everyone else, he was entirely naked, except for the horns and a black leather belt crisscrossing his chest. He was heavily tanned, which could hardly be discerned through the hair that covered his body in profusion, absent only here and there to accent how it flowed in channels over his body. His violet eyes had a new luster to them, whereas he had borne the slight illusion of the satanic when I had met him at the party, now he was the devil full blown—a devil of extreme sexuality and allure. Every inch of him exuded illicit sensuality. But what I couldn't take my eyes off was his cock. He was horse hung and was in full erection—and no doubt had taken something that would keep him so for a good long time.

I was growing more aware of my surroundings and started rattling my chains, trying to break free. But Donatien just walked up to me and pushed the stool off to the side now that my legs could more or less support my own weight. With a big grin on his face, he backhanded me smartly across the mouth, stunning me. Then his mouth, tongue, and teeth started to brutalize my pecs and nipples. He grabbed my head in both of his hands and went into another deep kiss on my lips. Once more his tongue pushed capsules down my throat. But instead of blacking out this time, the drug made me feel powerless, but increased my sensitivity to touch, and I also could feel my cock hardening and my ass canal loosening.

Still intent on struggling my way out of this, I bit him on the lip. He pulled away and gave me a startled look. Then he laughed, licked at his lip with his tongue, and backhanded me across the cheek again. My head snapped back, and he sank his teeth into my neck. I could feel him sucking at my blood. He only did this, though, long enough to demonstrate to me the totality of the power he had over me in this situation.

For the next half hour or more, Don played my body with his lips, teeth, and fingers. His mouth wound up on my cock, where he worked it in front until I thought I was going to explode. Just as I was ready to ejaculate, he'd slap my dick and hold me immobile until the need passed. But even though the urge to spout passed, the ache in my balls only increased. He let me rest briefly and then approached me from the rear, pulling my cock between my legs and alternating between working it and my asshole with his mouth. But when he sensed me tensing and about to shoot off again, he'd hold me off again.

All the time he was doing this, the rest of the men were working their way into a sexual frenzy. Right in front of me, I saw Doug bend a willowy young man forward over at the waist, enter him from behind in one long, continuous slide that had the young man panting and moaning, and begin pumping him in deep thrusts. While doing this, Doug was staring intently at me, and I had the sensation of him entering me rather than this anonymous young man. Another man was sucking the dick of Doug's partner, and in short order, yet another, heavily muscular man was riding Doug from behind as well. Doug threw his head back and laughed with pleasure.

The brazier had been moved from the altar, and a young man was stretched out on his back on the top of the stone top. Below him a beefy black man was spread-eagling the young man's legs and pumping away at his ass with a big, thick cock. A man covered in colorful tattoos was straddling the young man above and both were engaged in a vigorous 69 sucking. In one corner of the room, a completely hairless satyr was trussed up in a sling made of black leather straps and was being blown by one muscle man and fist-fucked by another, whose sweat glistened and whose wavy tattoos undulated in the light from torches placed along the walls.

A third man was languorously sucking the toes of the bald guy. And in another corner, another lithe, young man was strapped up to a hook by leather straps, and a tormenting satyr was flicking his back and buttocks with a riding crop and was inserting a thick dildo into his ass. The young man was writhing and twisting, but he was screaming repeated exclamations of "Yes!" and "More, deeper!" at the top of his lungs. Another muscular giant had a black satyr up against the wall. The giant was supporting the black man with beefy hands clutching his buttocks. The black man's legs were wrapped around the small of the giant's back and the giant was pounding away in the black man's ass with his club of a dick. A third man was fingering the giant's ass and working up his own cock with his hand.

I swiveled my head and saw, nearly at the edge of my peripheral vision, a satyr holding a flagon high over his head, letting wine stream out. Some of the wine managed to hit his mouth, but much of it was streaming down his face and onto and down his chest and belly. A second satyr was licking the wine off the torso of the first as it flowed down his glistening, marble-white skin. A third satyr was behind the first, his face planted firmly between the marbleized youth's butt cheeks. And, as I watched, he stood and took his engorged penis in his hand. His tool was fascinating; it was long and thin, with a rosy, bulbous helmet, and had a pronounced curve up toward his belly. It looked very much like an Oriental crescent sword. And, as he pierced the ass of the first satyr, I had the image of that bulbous helmet head dragging along the ass canal as it skewered its prey.

I swiveled my head back and saw that a tall, thin redhead was stretched out on his belly between me and the altar. A muscular blond lay full length on top of him, his arms atop the redhead's arms, the fingers of their hands entwined. Their heads were cheek to cheek; the blond's powerful thighs held those of the redhead's close together. Only the way that their fingers flexed and unflexed in a rhythmic fashion; that their faces shared an intense, yet faraway look; that the redhead moaned quietly; and that the blond's thighs twitched and his buttocks gently undulated revealed that the redhead was being deeply and tightly plowed.

I saw that the eyes of both the redhead and blond were focused on my own methodical taking under the ministrations of their dark, hairy master. Looking around the room, I could see that, in fact, nearly all of eyes of those around me were swimming in semen and fixed on what Don was doing to my body. I was the centerpiece of this party. No, obviously this was a ceremony of some sort rather than a party. I felt Don's teeth tighten around the root of my cock, and his index finger, thrust deep inside my ass, was rubbing relentlessly across my prostate, further engorging my cock and bringing me to the brink of coming under a sensation in my cock that I had never experienced before.

I heard a scream of ecstasy from one corner of the vault as the bald man in the sling shot arcs of cum on the chest of his tormentor, and from Doug as he arched his back to find the mouth of the man who was riding him and launched his load up the ass of the willowy young man he was servicing. The man strapped to the hook in another corner strained his head back and joined in the scream, as the dildo with which he was being prodded was pulled out, and his body was lifted off the ground by one dick entering him from behind and another joining the first as it entered him from in front. His body lurched and twitched and bobbed up and down against the piston motion of the two dicks slowly disappearing up his stretched asshole in a counterplunging drilling action. Legs planted firmly on the ground, the bulging-muscled torsos of the fucking duo leaned away from their shared toy, every vein bulging and rolling wildly and their mouths open in a tenor-baritone duet of intense pleasure.

The redhead stretched in front of me let out a loud groan, as the blond, going up on his knees, pulled the redhead's buttocks up with him and pumped him in five long, hard strokes with his throbbing cock before pulling out and spewing cum up the redhead's back. The blond fell back on his haunches, and the redhead came on his knees, turned, grabbed the blond by his calves, wishboned his legs, and plunged his dick into his partner's ass to where his strawberry pubic hair merged with vanilla fluff. As the blond arched his back and threw his head back and screamed in surprised pain laced with pleasure, the redhead started pumping away like mad.

All of this was too much for me; I had never imagined, not to mention seen, anything like this. In my mind, I thought I was going to die. But the drugs that were in me made me feel like I was observing this happening to someone else, not me, in spite of the physical sensations telling me that this was happening to me. And, unhindered this time, I shot off a load of semen down Don's throat. Don now lost focus on my cock and balls and moved back to in front of me. At his command, the chains on my wrists slackened considerably, and Don was pulling my head down to his crotch with both hands. The wet tip of his bulbous dick head pushed at my mouth, forcing it open. Gently, at first, he guided me in giving him suck and then, more insistently, he began to face fuck me, guiding my head in rhythm with his strong fingers. I gagged as he forced his enormous cock deeper toward the back of my throat. But when I thought I wasn't going to be able to take another breath, he pulled out of me, the chains jerked me back up to a standing position, and he moved around to behind me.

Don let out an animal howl, and we were receiving the full attention of the room now. Everyone disengaged from what they were doing and formed a circle around me, choosing their favorite vantage point from which to see me violated. Some were stroking themselves as they watched. Some were being stroked from behind by others, and Doug and a few others had their arms entwined around and their dongs up the asses of some of the younger satyrs. Still, while he was even then slowly fucking another from behind, Doug's eyes were locked on mine, and I felt he was sharing in everything that Don was doing in what was approaching the centerpiece of my ritual deflowering.

Standing right behind me, close to me, Don placed his palms on my hips and was gently stroking my butt cheeks with his thumbs. His breath was hot against the back of my neck, and I felt that huge tool of his running up the small of my back. He kissed me tenderly, and I trembled as I felt that bulbous head of his cock stroking its way down my back and into my crack.

CHAPTER THREE: PLANTING OF SEED RITUAL BEGINS

Donatien started lathering up my asshole with a glob of salve. He gave a command, and I found my legs being flipped up into the air and spread farther apart, with my hips suspended slightly above my head. Don walked around to in front of me. He was holding his gigantic cock in his hand and pulling at it in gentle, long strokes. He placed the bulbous head of his member at the entrance of my hole and rotated it around gently for some time. I whimpered quietly, paralyzed by fear of the anticipated but unknown. He told me to take a deep breath, and, as I did, he brutally entered me to the point where his dick helmet breached past my sphincter muscle. I threw my head back, my vision crowded by a sea of the muscled legs of my audience, and bellowed in pain and frustration, all of my veins bulging. I gritted my teeth, remembering that I had wanted this—that I had come for this—just not from Donatien. From Doug.

"The first breach of the virgin," the master announced in full voice, as a ripple of applause and murmurs of enjoyment and admiration fluttered through the circle of satyrs that surrounded me. I quickly realized, however, that writhing about would only push the assault ram deeper sooner, so I went rigid. Don whispered endearments at me, telling me to relax, that it would be far less painful if I relaxed and went with the flow. His hands ran across my belly, abs, and pecs, and he gently massaged me, helping me to relax.

As I relaxed, Don commented on how beautiful my body was and on how sure he was from my reactions that I must really be a virgin to the touch of man. His eyes sought Doug in the crowd around us and beckoned him over. I could hear Doug's cock slurp its way out of a young satyr's ass, as he extracted himself and walked over to us. Don expressed his pleasure at Doug's gift of my body for this ceremony and kissed him on the lips. From the murmurs in the crowd, I could tell this was a distinct honor. I heard Don tell Doug that, for his reward, he could join in the final ceremony on the altar, and Doug thanked him profusely and backed toward the crowd.

It was then, while I was relaxed, that Don pushed his cock into me two or three more inches. I started to tense again, but his helmet had found my prostate, and started rubbing back and forth on that, which produced sharp flashes of pleasure in my cock that were far beyond anything I had ever felt before. I moaned loudly.

"Furrowing the field," the master announced. The crowd voiced its congratulations.

"Oh, God, oh God," I moaned. I could feel precum bubbling up and out of my pisshole.

"Oh sweet baby," Don whispered to me. "You've never felt this before, have you?"

"Oh, God, no," I moaned back at him.

"Never realized it could feel this good, did you?" he pressed.

"Oh, God, oh, God. No!"

"Shall I stop or continue?" he asked. I hesitated and he pulled out from the prostrate and then rubbed back on to it with his dick head. The pleasure of the contact flooded back. I couldn't help my response.

"Oh, no, don't stop. Don't stop, please." I wailed.

He, of course, had no intention of stopping, but there were murmurs of approval from the crowd that I had begged for it, and he obviously was pleased at my acceptance of his power over me. He gave a command, and the tension was completely erased from the chains on my wrists, and I arched back. I didn't fall; however, because Don's strong hands supported me under my buttocks. He arched forward over me and his lips and teeth went to my nipples and abs. My throbbing cock was rubbing back and forth in the hair on his belly, and the combination of that sensation and the rubbing on my prostate made me come again.

"He came! The life-giving rains!" the master announced to the audience in jubilation, and there was another round of cheers and celebration.

The cock head continued on past the prostate another inch, and I was filled with pain.

"Plowing," the master declared. The tension in the room was electric.

"Oh, ah. A-h-h-h. Please." Another inch and, "Oh, God, no. Stop, please. You're splitting me. I can't—"

A command was given and my arms were pulled back up and Don was putting his mouth very close to my ear.

"Sssst," he was whispering insistently to me. "You must want it. You must want it for your own good. The ceremony is fixed. There is no alternative. I'm going to take you completely, one way or the other. But there are consequences if you don't want it."

"Oh, oh," I moaned. "It hurts. How much more? I can't take it."

Don laughed bitterly in my ear. "Can't take it? I'm only about half in myself now, and you are going to be taking it for hours—by cocks of all sizes."

"Oh, no, no, please," I cried. Another inch in and I lurched and moaned deeply.

"Plowing deeper," the master declared over my moans of pain. Both he and I felt the wetness that now lathered his cock.

"I confirm a new field. Virgin, unplowed ground!" he yelled in triumph, and he pulled his cock out of me to show all that it was smeared lightly in the blood of my ass canal. Excitement buzzed in the crowd.

"The ceremony is now validated and can proceed!" the master declared to a round of applause and louder buzzing and a great release of tension in the room. Obviously we had passed some sort of portal of the action.

He crouched and his lips and tongue went to my asshole. His ministrations were soothing, even if a little scary. I primarily was glad that he had stopped the plowing. When he came back up he leaned back down to me and put his mouth beside my ear.

"It's only this time you will feel the pain, I promise," Don said. "The drug I gave you will both increasingly loosen you and take away the pain. At some point there will only be pleasure. But for now the pain is necessary. You must be shown to have a virgin ass. The ceremony requires it. It also requires that I plow the field and plant the seed. After this first time, there will only be pleasure in it."

"Oh, oh," I whimpered. "But can you go more slowly?"

"I can mix more pleasure with the pain," Don answered. And to my groans and moans, he reentered me with his hard ramrod to where his cock helmet rubbed over my prostate again and slowly rotated his cock around in my ass canal with his hand wrapped around the root of his cock. That indeed, increased the pleasure, and my moans and sighs and grunts showed the increased satisfaction. Once more, upon command, the wrist chains released, and I arched back, which jutted my pelvis into Don's and forced his cock deeper up my canal, but this time not with nearly the pain I had experienced before.

"Tell me," Don commanded in a louder voice. "Tell me what you want me to do to you."

"OK, OK," I whimpered. "You can do it." But I gasped as the cock reached the deepest point it had attained earlier, a good six inches in.

"A second furrowing of the virgin fields! A sure harvest is a well-plowed field." Don announced to his adherents.

"Tell me. Tell me in your own words. Let me know you want it; that you consent to this taking of your virginity. To the dedication of your virginity to the master of this coven. Tell me." and them more softly into my ear. "It will happen regardless. There are dire consequences if you don't declare your willingness. I like you. I want you to pass the initiation."

He took the root of his cock in his hand and rotated the embedded end in my ass. My ass canal responded, widening to him and sending ripples of pleasant sensations through the muscles of my channel. This, in turn, made him gasp at the rippling across and around his embedded dick, and his eyes caught mine. And the flash in those violet eyes confirmed that we were on the brink of an action he could not control and that was inevitable. He was going to fuck me deeply. I knew that now. Nothing was going to prevent that. Doug would not be the first to reach my core. What the hell. I'd come here to be fucked. Curiosity had sealed my fate.

"Take me," I cried. The crowd bubbled over in exclamations of approval and awe.

"What do you want me to do?" Don screamed.

"Fuck me!" I cried. "Fuck me deep! Plow these fields and plant that seed. Please, now. Finish. Now. Fuck me hard, fuck me deep. You are the master of my body."

Don plunged into me that last four or five inches. I screamed in pain and he screamed in ecstasy.

"To the root! Reaching the good, virginal soil!" Don declared triumphantly, and the crowd roared its appreciation.

Immediately, he pulled nearly all the way out, and I sharply took in my breath, which exploded back out of me as he plunged back to the root.

"Oh, God, oh God, oh, God," I screamed, as he repeated this deep plunge several times, ending in the loud gush of "The seed of the master! The seed has been planted deep and true in virginal soil." The sensations of my innards being drowned in his semen washed over me. The cheers were deafening, reverberating around the stone walls.

CHAPTER FOUR: SHARING OF THE SACRIFICE RITUAL BEGINS

Relief poured over me along with Don's semen, which was bathing my insides. I thought I had survived the ritual. That it was all over now, that it would all get better. But nothing was happening. Well, nothing beyond the master satyr pulling out of me and marching around the circle, waving his still-engorged dong and exhibiting the mixture of his semen and my intestinal channel blood dripping from the gigantic organ. He had left me there, trussed up with my legs spread wide and cum and blood dripping out of my ass onto the floor. And then, when he had made a couple of victory laps to the appreciative comments of his coven, he returned to stand in front of me, positioning his pelvis between my suspended torso and spread legs.

He gave me a big, devilish grin, and declared. "You are worthy, sir. You have proven you are a virgin, and you have willingly and chastely given your virginity to the master of this coven. No part of you is a virgin now, and I have had the honor of taking you in every way. I am well pleased. Now, it is my duty to prove my manhood, my superior sustaining power to my men. The duty is over. The pleasure now begins. A well-plowed field is a productive field. The more seed planted vigorously and continuously, the more abundant the harvest!"

I barely had time to form my protest, when he pushed in between my legs, dripping, but very hard dick in hand, and slowly remounted me up to his root. As he had promised, though, the drugs had set in and the initial deflowering had passed. I felt more pleasure than pain now, as his man meat slid slowly and fully back into me and, for what seemed to be forever, pumped me both deeply and shallowly. His long, slender fingers dug into my butt cheeks, and he guided me back and forth on his long, thick ramrod. His mouth went to mine in a brutal kiss and then to my nipples, which he ravished with his lips and teeth. After an eternity, he came in another gusher, which he announced to the cheering crowd as a second seeding. He pulled out of me, came around behind me, and entered me again from behind. He wrapped his arms around my torso, bringing me very close into his chest, and he stroked and kneaded my pecs and nipples with his long, elegant fingers. We came together that time, which he was quick to point out to those encircling us as a third seeding enhanced by abundant rain.

At his signal then, the chains lowered me to the floor, minions unbound me, and Don continued to pump me in various positions, with me, now beyond pain and into my own zone of new-found ecstasy, increasingly finding and matching his rhythm and giving into the power and urgency of him. I was his now, and he knew it. We moved as one in the center of the floor, him enjoying my hairlessness and me enjoying the feel of his profuse, silky body hair. And when he came for the fourth time, with me fucking myself on the prone master and running my hands through his chest hair, and he slowly beat me off, while, entwined, we tenderly kissed.

When he had made me come again at last, he rose from me and signaled the rest of the men in the room, who descended on me, carried me over to and laid me on top of the altar, and, approaching me from every angle, filled my every orifice with dicks of varying lengths and thicknesses as I lay panting and moaning on the cold, hard stone.

"Feeding the masses from the abundant harvest," the master bellowed over the rutting masses.

I certainly hadn't counted on this part of the ritual, the throwing of the sacrifice to the mob. I was being covered in semen and came at least twice more that evening that I could remember. I had never produced semen this often or this fast. It must have been the drugs. But then, I'd never been in an orgy like this before.

I lay with my butt at the edge of one side of the altar and my head dangling off another end. The redheaded satyr was holding my head in his hands and face fucking my mouth from above. Someone was pouring wine on my chest and belly and licking me off there, paying special attention to my nipples and my navel. I felt my legs being wishboned and a cock entered my ass. I knew in an instant it was the satyr with the curved crescent sword cock, as a cock head was dragging across my prostate and kept dragging up my ass canal, changing the curve of the canal itself, giving me a sensation of my innards being stretched forward. I felt the weight of a man on my belly, and my own cock was entering a moist channel and being massaged by undulating walls as it slowly explored the depths of someone unknown. That unknown person was slapping his own cock on my abs and dry fucking me between my pecs as he worked his ass back and forth on my dick. Hands were deeply massaging my pecs and nipples; tongues were running over my legs. The thinner cocks at my mouth and anus were replaced by much thicker pieces. I gagged at getting past the helmet of a big, ropy-veined cock at my mouth and labored under a baseball bat-headed cock forcing purchase at my hole. When it was in several inches, I was turned on the altar, being spun on that big cock, and it continued pumping me from behind. My legs were being spread wide by multiple hands to give the batsman as wide a channel as possible. What he had been denied in length had been made up in breadth, and I was panting and moaning and grunting at the effort of taking him in. My cock was swallowed from below and yet another satyr was licking and sucking my balls. I was being faced fuck from below now. I reached around with my arms and placed my hands on this satyr's butt cheeks, only to find that he was being fucked from behind—the man with the extremely curved dick again. I followed the curve from the root of the dick with my hands until it had disappeared altogether and then I cuddled and pulled at the balls of the man sticking him. Now there were two satyrs on my chest and belly, one fucking the other.

At some point, I vaguely remembered four cocks pushing into me at once, two at either end, but by then I was close to blacking out again. The last separate phase of this ordeal that I remember was of the swirl of men falling back from the altar upon command and Doug coming up on the table, laying down behind me on the altar and gathering me tenderly in to him. His long, thick cock entered me and held there near the entrance until my sphincter muscle grabbed his bulbous dick head and pulled it in to where it rubbed against my prostrate. He let it rub there for a few minutes, as I trembled and moaned and sighed quietly within his arms. None of the rest of what had happened now mattered to me. The pain I had been through before was worth the reward of this pleasure. I could not have imagined that anyone could work my prostate as well as Don had just done, but Doug proved that to be wrong. I vaguely remember thinking that Doug had better be very careful that Don not find out that Doug quite possibly was the better lover.

The rest of crowd in the room was drifting away. This is what I had been fanaticizing about for the past week, entwined in Doug's strong arms, his horse-hung dick snaking up my ass canal, filling me to the limit. The drugs and the stretching and stuffing I had already experienced had taken away all of the pain. It was better that the pain was with someone else and pure pleasure was reserved for my long-anticipated fuck with Doug. All I felt now was Doug's need and urgency, his need to fill me with his hot, heavy cock. He was sighing and moaning with me now, pushing deeply into me, slowly and rhythmically pumping me with his manhood, sidesplitting me deeply as he had promised he would do. I suddenly knew that I was here because Doug wanted me, not because the master needed another sacrifice. And that thought made me fearful for Doug. I needed to guard against the overflowing feelings I had for Doug—at least as long as we were on display to the master's coven.

As my body calmed and went into a slow coordinated movement with Doug's rhythm, I felt him lift my leg high into the air, and, looking down my torso, I saw those violet eyes of the dark master, boring into me. I had to be careful now. I gave him a smile as if he owned me, as if he were my one and only lover, as if I were letting Doug fuck me only because the master had granted him this reward.

The master wrapped one hand around my engorged dick, which he gently stroked. His thumb was on my piss slit, probing and opening and closing it in a pleasurable rhythm. I watched, guarded but also completely lost in my gentle but relentless deep fuck from Doug, as the master's lips went to my leg. He tongued the surface from knee down to where the leg met the groin. This tickled and sent flashes of pleasure up and down my legs, but the real pleasure I was feeling was from Doug's cock in my ass canal, being rotated around and given short pumps at various depths by his long fingers that managed to manipulate his cock inside me, while rubbing an index finger on my prostate. His cock had a crock in it, and he was making me yip and moan by dragging his dick helmet around my ass canal walls.

"Rejuvenating the seed," I heard the master declare in a loud voice. My attention was jerked back from the sensations in my ass canal to those in my leg, as the crowd buzzed and a drum started a slow, but steady beat from the corner of the vault.

Donatien had found a pulsating vein on my leg in the crock of the groin, and I felt the pressure as he, first, deeply kissed me there, and, then, slowly sank his strong teeth into the vein and drank. For some reason, I didn't even notice and was feeling more pleasure from the sucking than pain. I was becoming woozy, though, which, no doubt, added to my lethargic attitude about Doug and Don's combined renewed assault on my body. If I had thought the thorough deflowering of my body at the hands of the satyr master was to be all there was to this ceremony, I obviously had been badly mistaken. I thought I heard a low, but sustained murmuring of the crowd of men whose close presence around the altar I felt more than saw. And a drum started a slow beat somewhere off in a corner of the vault.

The fear of being drained of blood slowly worked its way into my brain. Donatien had sucked on a vein earlier in this ordeal as a signal of his total control over me in this place, but I hadn't

41

thought about the ramifications of that to this point. Sensing my reaction and the reintroduction of a higher level of fear, Don pulled away from me and whispered reassuringly to me, "This is where the ritual parts ways on the virgin's declared willingness as opposed to a rape," Don said to me. "We drink sparingly from the willing; we drain the unwilling. Relax. I see that Doug is giving you deep pleasure. Go with those sensations. Never fear." And he returned to sucking gently at my leg, which began to feel numb.

Doug was kissing me deeply on the neck, and then I felt his teeth break into my carotid and he, like Don, was sucking my blood. A flash of concern went through me, wondering if Don knew that he was sharing this rejuvenation with Doug. Strangely enough, this was increasing my own pleasure, and I decided that Doug could look after himself. As Doug sucked, I could feel his dick lengthen and thicken, and he was plowing farther into me than anyone else had gone this evening. He must be over eleven inches into me. I'd never heard of a fuck this deep. But, as far as I could care, this could go on forever. His hand was roughly rolling and kneading one of my nipples, and his own moans had increased in intensity and had an animal edge to them.

I wondered briefly if someone like him could lose control and fuck someone else to death. If so, I was weakening and wouldn't be able to do a thing about it. The fingers of his other hand left the rotation of his dick and the stroking of my prostate, and I felt them going to the entrance of my ass and pushing the opening even farther apart. At least another half inch of his dick entered me. He had been holding something in reserve. I moaned loudly and groaned and grunted, and wondered just how far into my intestines a baseball bat could go. If this was leading to death, it must be one of the most pleasurable ways to go.

I felt Don detach his teeth from the vein in my leg and tongue his way up to my balls. He sucked those momentarily, and then I felt his lips at the underside of my cock, right where it entered into the ball sac. He was holding my cock up against my belly and was licking the bulging vein there that was pumping blood into my engorged cock.

"The purest of the pure." he declared to the coven, and then he sliced his teeth into the vein, and, whether from what Doug's rod was mining or Don's lips were sucking, I came in three gigantic spasms. Don had sensed that I was ready to come and had his mouth over my dick to accept my hot semen.

"The last of innocence," the master declared to the room, semen bubbling out of his mouth. "The essence of the sacrifice; the mingling of the purest of the life juices. The end of the ritual!" The room erupted into loud cheers and screams. He returned to gently sucking blood from the root of my throbbing cock, Doug shot off twelve drug-induced inches deep, deep inside me, and I heard the drum pick up the beat and sound of its tempo, as I slowly drifted into unconsciousness.

CHAPTER FIVE: PROCURER'S PAYBACK; SIDETRACKING A VIRGIN

When I awoke, it was nearly dawn, and I was back at the gym parking lot, fully clothed and lying on the back seat of my car, but aching and hurting in every nook and cranny of my body. I was still a little woozy from the drugs and the loss of blood and moved with great lethargy and moans that were completely different from those that Don and Doug had dragged out of me earlier in the evening. I'm sure that much of what had happened in that stone vault was subsequently lost to me, and I even began to question how much of it was real and how much of it was my vivid imagination at work.

I found that, for the life of me, I couldn't even remember now where the party had been; I didn't have the foggiest notion how we had gotten there. But I could feel the pain in my ass canal and could feel it stretched so wide that I doubted it would ever return to the tightness it had before this repeated plowing, a fact that wasn't all that unpleasant for the many men I subsequently tried out in search of the level of pleasure that Doug had given me in that last glorious side split.

I found a note on my dashboard. It was from Doug. I had passed my initiation with flying colors, he said. The master had been very pleased. And if I was interested in joining his coven, I should leave a note pasted to his locker in the gym. If not, though, I would never see Doug again and should not try to find him. He wouldn't come back to work out at that gym unless I joined the coven; he was not permitted to have sex with other men outside the coven. He noted that he had shared women outside the coven with those he'd initiated before but that he didn't think he could trust himself with me in such a situation. He admitted that I had been the best fuck he'd ever had.

Left with the note was a small bottle of capsules. A handwritten tag on the bottle said, "The answer to a twelve-inch cock. Take two." I opened the bottle and counted the capsules, wondering even then who I might deem worthy of a surprisingly deep fuck—or whether I'd save them all to slip into the meal of some hunky man I picked up in a bar and took home.

I might be the curios type, but no one could say that it was impossible to fully satisfy my curiosity. I didn't leave a note for Doug. I still found him maddeningly attractive, and there were moments for some time that the memory of his masterful cock and searching lips and hands filled my thoughts as fully as his cock had filled and stretched my very core, although, yes, I did get a capsule-induced twelve-inch fuck from a wildly surprised and appreciative hunk from time to time during the next few weeks. But, now that I was away from that stone vault, I could accept that Doug had cold bloodedly and purposely procured me as a virginal sacrifice to his master in some dark satanic ritual. And I could see now that the privilege he had received of sharing me with the master—albeit after the master had taken all forms of my male-on-male virginity—in the highest ritual was just a reward for Doug's having found, cultivated, seduced, and delivered me— without any thought for what I might think or have to say about it.

Doug was probably out cultivating another sacrificial lamb right now. I found I could not forgive him for that, even though I seemed no worse for the experience after I'd rested for a week. Within a couple of weeks, I noted that Doug's locker at the gym had been reassigned to a pudgy executive who looked well beyond ready for retirement, even though he was still randy enough to give me a few purposeful looks.

I went on to experiment with my sexuality with other men—to the surprise of several who thought it was my charms alone that had coaxed their cocks to nearly a foot long. But nothing I did in the ensuing weeks approached the wildness of when my virginity was first sacrificed—nor the satisfaction of that first deep fuck I had gotten from Doug. And that's why I set out to find and compromise Doug, both to pull him from the coven and to experience that incredible dick inside me once more.

It took me over eight months of intense searching through all of the gyms in and around the city before I found Doug, but I did find him. I stayed in the shadows and watched him as he put the moves on a young, Middle Eastern university student who seemed far more oblivious to what was going on than I had been when Doug seduced me. He also was chatting up the women in the gym, and I saw his lack of struggle when a buxom brunette had him up against a wall near the passage to the locker rooms and was exploring his basket with her hands.

I laid out my plans carefully. I determined what evenings Doug regularly attended the gym and then scoped out the evenings that the student and the buxom brunette attended the gym when Doug wasn't there. I also followed Doug home from the gym until I struck on a night when he went out to Donatien's mountainside mansion out in the suburbs. I made note of the address of and directions to the mansion. I now knew where the coven met. That part of the plan settled, I turned my attention to Doug's friends at the gym.

I started to attend the gym on nights the student and brunette were there but Doug wasn't, and I put some moves of my own on the two in separate campaigns. The brunette fell first. She was the very, very friendly type, who turned out to work on her back on the side for money, and it wasn't long before she had me up against the wall by the passage to the locker rooms and her hand down the front of my gym shorts. She liked what she found, and we finished the evening with her sucking me off in the backseat of my car and me telling her that cars inhibited me and I was sure she'd like the goods even better in her own bedroom. Curiosity got to her with little difficulty. I invested two of the capsules Doug had given me, and the brunette had the deepest, most enjoyable fuck of her life. She was all over me to repeat the performance, which I said I'd do if she did me a little favor by setting up a threesome when I wanted it arranged. A threesome suited her just fine, even with my stipulations, and she was even more pleased with the money I stuffed in her ample bra.

The olive-skinned Middle Eastern student was a harder sell. He obviously had no idea he had homosexual tendencies, and it took me several weeks of dropping the soap in the shower and inadvertently rubbing up against him on the gym floor to evoke his interest. But I had already proven my desirability to other men, and eventually one day he accepted a ride home, with a side trip to my place, which started with a mild Mickey in a drink that loosened him up and then to a complete collapse of his inhibitions.

After the effects of his drink started settling in, he perched himself on my kitchen island counter and agreed with me that it was entirely too warm in my apartment. No sooner had we stripped off our T-shirts and I came in close to him than he had his hands running through my now regrown chest hair, and we were locked in a tender kiss. I worked my lips down his smooth chest, six-pack, and flat belly, and sucked on his cock through his shorts and briefs until the material was transparent, his nice cock

49

was apparent, and he declared that he would explode if I didn't stop—and then lamented that he'd be a wreck if I did stop.

I stripped off my own shorts and briefs and came up on the island on my knees in front of him and let him suck me without having to strain through fabric. I could tell from his clumsy, but still very nice, efforts that he was a virgin to this sort of thing, and I considered the rest of what we did that night as saving him from Donatien's coven.

I stripped off his wet clothes, with him agreeing in a fog that they now needed to be dried before he could use them, turned him over on the top of the island, and tongued up his ass for several minutes before reaching over for the butter off the other kitchen counter and lathering up his ass nicely.

I was gentle with my first entry, far more gentle that either Don or Doug had been with me, and I stopped at every stage of the way to allow him to adjust to my length and width, which, even when not enhanced by Doug's capsules, were quite enough to put me into the highly desirable category at the gay bars I had started to frequent since my initiation by the coven. I was kneeling on my calves on the island top, and the student faced me, with his legs straddling my thighs. This gave me ready access to his lips to assure him this was true romance and to his nipples when he arched his back in the pain merging into pleasure of my cock slowly skewering his ass. I had given him the full prostate attention with my cock helmet, and his dick was just as hard as it was going to get and was bubbling precum when I slipped a couple of inches farther in, wrapped my hand around his rod, and started stroking inside him.

He complained of the pain and was panting hard when I pulled him two inches closer into my lap, but he forgot all about the pain when I put my thumb on his piss slit and started flexing it open and closed. I took my other hand, wrapped it around the base of my cock and gave him a taste of ass canal wall rubbing. I discovered that this was the key to his response mechanism, as he went wild, flung his arms around me, went into a deep kiss and started moving his hips against me, which pulled him onto my dick far enough that I didn't have any root to rotate. The thumb-on-piss slit trick worked as well, as he shot his load up between our pulsating stomachs and into the cleavage of our rubbing pecs.

I finished him by lifting him off the counter and frog-marching him over into the living room. I draped him over the back of an upholstered chair, folded one of his knees up to the top of the chair to gain added access, and ran my dick up into him several inches. He no longer was complaining about the pain, but he also may have lost some interest when he got his own rocks off, so I held out of him enough to get a grip on the root of my cock and gave him a repeat of the rotating rod game. He fell apart in ecstasy again, which allowed me to ram all the way up into him and pump off my own rocks.

Fifteen minutes of the romantic canoodling and mutual fondling of balls that he seemed to enjoy, followed by a vigorous twenty minutes of side splitting on the living room carpet that had him writhing with enthusiasm and toasting me in some exotic language, and a quick shower with us soaping and jerking each other off again, and he was ready to be driven home, no doubt to a dull, obedient spouse who only responded to the missionary position.

He proved to be a nice, simple lay, but nothing special. The most important thing was that he no longer was a virgin, and it might take Doug several more weeks visiting the gym I'd found him at to discover that his current prey didn't qualify for the coven's specifications. He may have been a virgin to male attentions before he sat on my kitchen island counter, but he certainly wasn't a virgin now.

CHAPTER SIX: SPRINGING THE PAYBACK HONEY TRAP

Now I could put the ultimate part of the plan into operation. The brunette was good at what she did. On the date she specified, she had everything set up, and all of her directions, as I had outlined to her, were followed explicitly. We were in her darkened bedroom, stretched out on the bed. I was the one in the black mesh stockings and the spiked heels. I had shaved my legs, just like the coven liked them. I also had made sure I was buried in pillows so that my torso and face were covered in the deeper shadows in the room. The brunette was straddling me, doing a very good job of pretending that two cunts were being rubbed together in ecstasy—when, in actual fact, she was getting a deep fuck that she seemed to be enjoying immensely.

She had told Doug that she wanted to surprise a girlfriend of hers. That she understood he was known for having a monster cock, and that her girlfriend enjoyed taking monster cocks up the ass. It was her friend's birthday, and she wanted to surprise her with a threesome. Doug was intrigued with the idea and agreed to enter the dark apartment through the door the brunette would leave open, to shed his clothes in the living room, and to quietly enter the bedroom and plow the girlfriend's ass while the brunette serviced her from above. Then he could fuck both women together if he wanted to.

Doug arrived exactly when and as told. He'd popped his capsules, so both women were going to get the ride of their lives. As he entered the bedroom, he could barely make out the pair on the bed. But he saw the back of the brunette he knew, her hair flowing down her back and her pelvis rubbing up and down on the figure under her. The figure under her had nice legs, accentuated by enticing black mesh stockings and stiletto heels. Her legs were wide apart, knees bent on the edge of the foot of the bed, and Doug could see that her ass was wide open to him.

He came up to the humping figures. To let the brunette know he was there, he put his arms around her, covering her ample breasts with his hands, and jiggled her quarter-sized nipples while nuzzling his face into her neck. The brunette giggled and then took in a gulp of breath, as she felt Doug's now-huge cock run up between her shoulder blades.

Two impossibly hung men. Her resolve faltered for a brief moment, while she considered not fulfilling her part of the deal in trade for the possibility of having twelve inches run up her from both sides at the same time, but a deal was a deal, and if she played it right she might eventually get both of them in her simultaneously anyway.

The brunette turned her face to Doug and gave him a deep kiss and then whispered in his ear to go ahead, that she'd help control her girlfriend.

So Doug moved back, sliding his dick off the brunette's back, and carefully putting his hands on the bottom figure's ankles, he lifted the legs up and away from him, rolling the two figures so that the butt rolled up on the one with the stockings and further exposed "her" asshole to him.

There was an exclamation from the top of the bed, which was muffled by the pillows, and the stockinged legs flinched. The brunette soothed her friend.

"It's OK, Suzy." the brunette cooed. "It's my birthday surprise to you. A hot, heavy cock from a real hunk, right up your ass. Just the way you like it. Just lay there and enjoy it, honey. Debbie's taking care of everything. You'll simply drool when you see how hunky the man is who plowed you."

More muffled noises from the top of the bed, but "Suzy" obviously didn't object to this surprise. Doug went down on his knees at the foot of the bed, running his hands down the stockinged legs to the thighs and holding the butt in the presentation mode. The brunette's butt draped down to where Doug couldn't get a look at "Suzy's" twat, but he could clearly see the asshole. It gaped a bit. It was quite apparent that "Suzy" indeed liked to be plowed in the ass. That was all the confirmation

Doug needed. His nose and mouth went to her crack. She was lightly perfumed in an enticing scent.

Doug kissed the hole, and the butt twitched. He rimmed it with his tongue, and the stockinged legs trembled. He inserted and flicked his tongue, and he could hear a moan that was distinct from the considerable moaning and sighing the brunette was doing, and my cock gained interest, thickened, and marched farther up the brunette's cunt. If the capsules and Doug's ministrations combined well, the brunette would enjoy at least four more inches of me before her role was done.

Doug went to work seriously in moistening and opening the asshole. When he was satisfied, he stood and placed the head of his dick at the entrance to my ass. He rotated it around in what was a remembered way as he slowly worked it in the first inch. I moaned for him appreciatively and moved my ass for him to help him gain purchase and to show him I was interested and ready for him.

I thought the game was going to be up then, though, as he lifted one of my legs, flipped the shoe off, and started to roll the stocking off my leg. In the heat of the moment he either didn't realize my leg was as heavily muscled as it was or he thought he'd encountered a woman runner and weight lifter, but it probably turned out to be a really good thing that I'd shaved the legs and painted my toenails. He then began kissing my feet, ankles, and calves and as far up the leg as he could get without losing the position of his dick helmet in my ass. Where his lips couldn't reach, he sent his hand, and his fingers continued from my leg to my ass, and, as he had done with me on the coven altar, he inserted three fingers, at nine, twelve, and three o'clock, between the sides of his shallowly emplaced cock and the sides of my ass canal. He slowly worked his fingers in two inches and spread them. His dick followed along behind, between the fingers, and he was in two inches. This was a maddeningly inventive and sensual entry plan that, I'm sure, worked equally well for men and woman. I let him know I appreciated the performance by groaning and moaning in falsetto and lurching my butt toward him as best I could to take him in another half inch.

He met the challenge by digging deeper with his fingers, spreading and gaining an extra inch of buried cock. He was well beyond my sphincter muscle now, which pulled him on another inch, and he withdrew his fingers. I showed him how much I was enjoying this by working my free foot, the one on the leg not being run up the left side of his magnificent chest, and the one still in stockings and heels, to where I could push the toe up under his ball sac and apply pressure behind the root of his cock.

Doug exclaimed and laughed aloud. Then he grunted as I started running the toe across his perineum in search of his asshole. Then he yelped and pulled my foot out from between his legs and flipped the shoe off. Grabbing both of my legs at the calves, he wishboned me and ran his cock into me at six or seven inches and began a slow and shallow fuck of my ass. I had hoped he wouldn't notice that I was equipped with a prostate—and, to tell the truth, I didn't know whether that even could be discerned by a cock in full heat. But, by chance, I had encouraged him to push even deeper. He slowly mined the depths, pumping me at several levels. At eight inches, he brought my legs back to run up between his now-heaving chest and the brunette's back. I had been playing with the brunette's tits, just as she was playing with mine, and I just got my hands away in time for Doug to take over. He must have been rougher on her tits than I was, because she was yipping and moaning and groaning and bouncing a bit on my skewer, which went to eleven inches under her attention.

After a few minutes, he wishboned my legs again so that he could bury his meat to nine inches, where he spent some time in an energetic slide in and slide out fuck. It seemed like this was as far as he was going to go, not having any idea of my tolerances, but in the highest and most muffled voice I could manage and still get the idea across, I yelled, "Deeper, harder. Debbie said you were a hung stud. Feed me some meat."

With a flair of anger, he pushed immediately to the eleven-inch level and to alternating long and short strokes.

"Deeper, deeper," I cried, and the brunette was writhing and throwing herself about now, as I was plowing her deeper too.

"You asked for it, Babe," Doug muttered, as he dipped more than twelve inches. I was expanding and contracting my ass muscles just to let him know that I could play a good game to.

Doug let loose of my legs again, and grabbed for the brunette's tits, trying to keep her from throwing herself around so much. While one hand squeezed a tit, the other moved down her belly, in search of her cunt, ready to play with her there as well.

And that was when he learned there was a dick up her cunt, not another cunt rubbing against hers.

Luckily I had reached twelve inches inside the brunette by then and was bathing her deeply with semen, my ejaculation coming at the precise minute that Doug encircled the root of my cock with his fingers in wonder of what he had found down there.

"Now!" I yelled at the brunette. "Off now! As agreed."

The brunette dutifully rolled off from between us and over the side of the bed. She hobbled over to a lounge chair, turned the lights up a notch at a nearby switch, draped herself in the chair, and watched the two hung studs go at it while she rubbed her clit with a very experienced finger.

And then it was just Doug and me. I stretched on the bed and him posed over me, in shock, his cock twelve inches up my ass. As I was prepared for this, I was faster off the mark then he was. I wrapped my legs around his ass, holding him inside me, while I pulled him onto the bed. Rolling him with my body, I got him on his back, with his legs off the foot of the bed. I was straddling him, still encasing his cock, and I planted my hands on his shoulders at the arm pits, while I wildly bounded up and down on his cock, driving him even deeper into me.

"What?" He was crying. "Kevin? What? How? Why? Stop that. Get off me!"

"No," I exclaimed. "Pump me. Fuck me. Deeper. Deeper. Plaster me deep with your cum."

"Oh, God! No, I can't," he cried.

But I didn't listen to him. I pulled his torso up to me and parted his lips with mine and went into a full, French kiss. Our tongues met, and slowly he succumbed to me, as I continued to fuck myself on his cock in deep, shallow strokes. His head flopped back and my lips and teeth went to his nipples. His hands went to my butt cheeks and squeezed hard.

He was moaning and groaning, fighting me, but with ever weaker resolve. And eventually, he let out an animal sound and overpowered me. Rather than retreating, though, he pushed me over on my side, during which his dick was extracted from my ass. But he went on his side as well, and nestling my butt into his groin, he lifted my leg high into the air and entered me again. This time he stopped briefly at my prostrate to get my cock bubbling precum again and then slid deep into my ass. We were in his favorite position. I had won. He was mine.

I hummed quietly to myself as he deep fucked me to the thirteen-inch level. He was holding my flat, panting belly firmly into his lap with his free hand, sliding the black stocking off with the other and running his hand up and down my smoothly shaved legs and deep kissing my mouth. I heard him sigh in resignation as he came deep inside me, lathering my insides once more with the powerful spurts of his man juice.

We lay there for an eternity. Both of us full of drugs that held us at full erection. Doug allowed me to drop my leg, but he stayed encased deeply inside me. His hand now was playing with my long, thick cock and my balls.

"You know why I did this, don't you?" I whispered into Doug's neck.

"The coven. Revenge for the coven experience. I can't go back now. I've had sex with a man outside the coven."

"Right," I answered. "But it was for me too. I want you inside me. This seemed the only way. I wasn't going to join the coven."

Doug laughed quietly. "But I like variety," he said.

"So do I," I replied. And danger, if it comes to that.

"I could just ignore that this happened, and continue with the coven, you know," Doug countered.

"Probably not," I replied. "I know where the mansion is. I'm sure I could convince the master you'd fallen off the wagon." And then I told him the address of Donatien's mansion, and Doug rewarded me with another dry laugh.

"It was getting a little dangerous there for me anyway," Doug whispered. "Donatien was losing position as I was gaining it. He could only see that as a threat."

"I noticed," I said. "No one, including Don, made love to me that night like you did. I'm sure he noticed."

A cough was heard from across the room. "If you boys aren't using that big long cock, I know where you can find a case for it." The brunette who had helped me and who politely stayed off to the side, enjoying the show, as I seduced Doug and he fucked my brains out was pleading her case.

"So, would you be up for our hostess?" I asked Doug.

"I'm still very hard up your ass," he laughed. "Does it feel like I've lost interest in a good fuck?"

"OK, she's was very good about this," I said. "Let's give her a thrill."

We bounced off the bed, and Doug asked, "Cunt or ass?" as we strode toward a surprised, but very pleased buxom brunette.

"Ass, I guess," I answered as we got to the chaise lounge and lifted the brunette up on her feet. "I've plowed her cunt already tonight. She probably will appreciate the change."

The brunette looked like she would very much appreciate the servicing by two luscious studs no matter who stuffed what where.

Doug grabbed the big, square pillow off the back of the chaise lounge and plunked it down on the bottom edge of the lounge. He then sat down on it, with his feet on the floor, and directed the brunette to sit in his lap, facing him. She did so, and Doug positioned his erect phallus at the entry of her cunt, held her up under her breasts with his strong hands, and slowly lowered her onto his totem pole.

The brunette gasped and moaned and sighed and gave little yipping sounds as she slowly descended his rod.

"Oh my, oh yes. Oh, my God. No, it's okay. I've already had one this size up me tonight. Go ahead. Oh, yes. Oh, Baby. Oh God. Pump me. Fuck me deep. Oh, Baby."

When she was fully skewered, Doug began to lift and push her down, alternatively, fucking her deeply, as she had requested. The brunette's neck loosened, and her head flopped around. She was clearly enjoying this.

I came up close behind her and let my cock run up her spine just as Doug had done earlier, and brought my hands around her and worked her tits just as he had done. And she moaned as deeply for me as she had for him. This time, however, her chest was pushed into Doug's, and I was playing with his tits as well. I got their nipples on both sides in line and brushed them back and forth across each other, and both rewarded me with sighs and moans. My chin rested on the brunette's shoulder and Doug and I kissed each other deeply.

"You, you. Now you," the brunette whispered in my ear insistently.

So I moved back, tilted the brunette's pelvis up and tongued her asshole briefly. She had used the same enticing perfume on her ass that I had to fool Doug. Then I slowly entered her ass, while she cried out in pain and ecstasy, telling me in no uncertain terms not to stop pushing up her ass no matter how she screamed until she had all twelve inches of both of us. I obliged, and once rooted, both Doug and I moved our cocks in and out and around, until, in a flopping frenzy, the brunette achieved her orgasm, which was well timed with Doug's ejaculation.

The brunette was cooing when I pulled out of her, pushed her and Doug onto their backs on the chaise, spread Doug's legs, and entered him. I didn't stop to rub his prostate or anything else, but pushed in a good six inches, before he had the presence of mind to scream.

The brunette started laughing and pinned Doug to the chaise with her ample bosom. Doug fought me with his powerful legs, but I already was deeply encased, and pushed in farther with each of his lurches.

"God, you'll split me. Get off," Doug yelled.

"Don't be a baby," I said, as I pushed to ten inches. "I saw you get fucked at the coven affair, and you were liking it then. This is all part of the plan."

"Ohhh, Awww," he screamed as I pushed in eleven inches and then started a furious, long-stroked pumping action.

Doug heaved up furiously, and the brunette went off one side of the chaise, and Doug and I went off the other side. Doug and I landed in a side-split position, with me still embedded, and I lifted his leg high in the air and drove the full twelve inches in. He let out a cry, but that soon subsided into a whimper, which changed to a sensual moan and a purring sound deep in his throat, as I pumped him in the ass with long and deep strokes and worked his tool and balls with my hand. In short order, he was moving in rhythm with me, and I was learning why he liked this position so much. When I came, our lips were locked together and our tongues were dueling. Our hostess turned out the lights and collapsed on her bed with a very satisfied sigh, while we lay there on the floor next to the chaise lounge the rest of the night, with me buried deep inside Doug, as the drugs wore off. I felt he was truly mine now.

CHAPTER SEVEN: IT AIN'T OVER UNTIL IT'S OVER

The next two months were the most blissful that I had ever had—or, the foreboding oppressive thought, quite possibly that I would ever again have. I moved in with Doug, and we freely shared everything in life, most especially our cocks. He was enough for me. I didn't need women or other men now. I was ready to settle down for a life of my butt nestled into his lap. Beyond an occasional inexplicable feeling of panic, I didn't give another thought to Donatien or his coven during that period of bliss. But I should have done so.

One night we turned in early after an exhausting day of tennis followed by a vigorous workout in the gym. We had explored each other's bodies with soap and water during a long, drawn-out shower, followed by toweling each other off and a naked tussle on the bed, with me winning and, as a reward, pulling Doug into my lap, facing me, as I knelt on the bed watching the expressions of desire in his face as he slowly skewered his ass on my cock. He was arched back, and I arched forward, wrapping my arms around his torso, finding his nipples with my lips and teeth, when I was suddenly jerked up and out of him from behind.

The bedroom was swarming with big, beefy men, stripped to the waist. Doug was hauled off of the bed and over into a corner, where several of the men started beating him with their fists. He was fighting back and landed a couple of good punches of his own, but there were too many of them, and they were too strong for him. In short order, they had beat him senseless and were dragging him out of the room.

Meanwhile, other men had strapped my hands together with a leather thong at the wrists and had tied off the other end on the brass slats at the top of the bed. I was yelling and screaming, but no one was paying any particular attention to me.

All the time this was going on, a huge, black man was standing almost motionless in the middle of the room, supervising the action with just a few hand gestures here and there. He was a monster of a man, more than seven feet tall and built like a footfall fullback. He was a handsome devil with dreadlocks that reached his shoulder.

When they had silenced Doug and hauled him out of the room by his arms, his head dangling and his feet dragging on the floor, the black monster turned and grinned down on me where I lay on my back on the bed, my arms tied above my head.

"And what shall we do with you, my lovely?" he teased me with in a thick, baritone Jamaican accent. "I know. You can be my bitch for tonight." With that, he pulled off his pants and stood there in all his oversized glory. He had balls and a humongous dong that more than matched his beefy seven-foot physique. His gigantic nipples were pierced with golden rings as was the seemingly tennis-ball sized helmet of his half-hard cock.

"You're from the coven, aren't you?" I cried, suddenly realizing how vulnerable Doug and I had been to the wrath of Donatien the past two months.

"Of course," he said, as he mounted the bed, making the bedsprings groan under his weight, and sat astride my chest. I felt like he was going to crush me with his powerful thighs.

"Then you can't touch me," I said. "I'm not of the coven. You can't have sex outside the coven."

"Ah, but there you are wrong," the Jamaican said with a laugh. "The master considers you part of the coven, and I was, regrettably, absent the evening of your initiation. He has specifically told me I can take you. That is my reward for bringing the renegade member back."

"But it's not Doug's fault!" I cried. "I tricked him. I made him untouchable in the coven."

"Enough, bitch," the black monster demanded. "Suck me to hard. Prepare me for the fuck of your life." With that, he pulled my head up by the hair, and pressed the head of his cock between my lips.

"Suck me good, bitch," he demanded, "Or you'll be sorry. You thought your Doug was well hung. Well, I have the thickest and longest dick in the coven, and I have access to the same drugs Doug does, and you are going to be fucked deeper than you have ever been before and in more ways than you can count."

I dutifully kissed and tongued and sucked on the Jamaican's cock as it grew to astronomical length and thickness. Meanwhile, one of the other men still in the room prepared my ass with his tongue and, apparently, with added salve. At length, the Jamaican leaned back and inserted a beefy finger in my ass and finger fucked me deeper than most men could do with their cocks. He rubbed hard on my prostate, and as precum was bubbling out of my cock and I was moaning loudly, he gave permission to one of the men in the room to suck me off, which he did intensely and quickly.

And then the Jamaican came off my back, flipped me around on my stomach, and raised me onto my knees. I felt the cold metallic feel of the golden ring in his cock helmet at my asshole and he was pushing into me. He was splitting me as I never was split before. I could not take him in. It was going to be impossible. At his command, however, there were hands on both of my legs and on my belly, and my legs were being drawn far apart and suspended at the level of the Jamaican's groin. Other hands were drawing my butt cheeks farther apart. And then he was in. I screamed bloody murder as he slowly rose up my ass canal. Heavy, roped veins running down his cock rippled across the walls of my canal, causing the channel to go into wild contractions. The Jamaican gave another command, and one of the men was above me, pushing his thighs in a kneeling position under my chest and forcing his cock into my mouth—forcing me to suck on him to stifle my screams. His hands were on the back of my head, holding me in place.

Deeper, deeper the Jamaican plowed, opening my canal wall to and almost beyond the limit. He didn't brutalize me, though. He pushed in slowly, and, although Doug had never been this thick, he had prepared me so that I could withstand this— barely. He was in farther now than anyone, including Doug, had ever gone. At his command, my legs were lowered on the bed, and then he gathered them in between his strong thighs. I could feel his pubic hair mashed against my butt cheeks, so I knew he was in to the hilt. He commanded the man with his cock in my mouth to clear out, and I was free of him now, laying flat on the bed, gasping for air, and all of my attention focused on the gigantic club, with its rippling veins, reaching up for my stomach from my asshole.

The Jamaican lowered his massive chest on my back, and he enfolded me in a close embrace. His ham-hocked hands came under me and covered my pecs and nipples. He nibbled on my ear and kissed me in the crook of my neck. His dreadlocks covered my face. I was panting heavily, trying to contain the pain, slowly adjusting to him inside me.

"You've got one sweet ass, Mon," he whispered in my ear. "Just as the master promised. We're going to be great friends, you and I. There aren't too many who can be trained to take what I have to give. Doug made a good start on training your sweet ass to my needs."

I whimpered and moaned, but he could feel me relaxing, adjusting to him.

"Kiss me, Mon," he whispered in my ear. "Relax, and don't fight it."

I turned my head to the side and met his lips. He pushed his tongue in and took control of my mouth, stifling my scream as his hips started to undulate and his dick came to life inside me. He pumped me slowly and shallowly, at least at first. Waves of pain rolled over me, and I felt the golden ring dragging along my ass walls, mining even deeper into me. He must have tired of this position, because, in one coordinated move, he slowly spun my body on his cock and changed his own position so that I now was face up on the bed, and he was at a right angle below me, my legs arched over his hips. He was T-squaring my ass with his rod so that the top of his cock was now running up the side of my ass canal. The thick veins in his cock now gave their attention to a whole new canal surface. He grabbed my hips with his hands and moved my ass up and down on his pole.

Just when I'd become accustomed to this position, he dragged me up to my knees on the bed, facing the headboard, with his big mitts dug into my pecs. We scooted closer to the head of the bed to give me more play on the leather strappings. He widened the stance on his thighs, pushing mine out, which opened me up more to his relentlessly pumping cock. He held me to him with one arm crossing my chest and a hand spread on one of my breasts. The other hand went down to my belly and then to my cock and balls.

The pain was still there, but my own desire was growing, and some pleasure was breaking through. It was a thrill that I was handling a cock of more than thirteen inches and with the thickness almost of a normal wrist. The strokes became longer and more insistent, and the Jamaican was breathing heavy. He pitched me forward and down, so that my weight was supported on the mattress on my shoulders, my head now getting a good view of the club pounding my ass. He held me suspended with his hands on my thighs, holding my legs up and out, and he jack-hammered his pile driver down into my ass. After growing tired of this position, the Jamaican stood up on the bed, bringing me with him. He lifted my feet out and away and I placed them on the top of the brass headboard, lodged against the balls at the corner. My torso was stretched forward by the leather bonds binding my wrists. His pelvis was under me, he held me by the hips, and he pumped up into me from below like a mighty piston. He was right. I was losing count of the separate positions he was ravishing me with.

We were both panting and moaning and groaning and yelling to each other how great a fuck this was. There was little pain for me now; I was lost in the action of the huge sausage powering its way in and out of my ass. His dreadlocks were whipping around my head.

The bed frame collapsed under us, and the brass headboard fell apart, freeing my hands from being lashed to the bed, although my wrists were still bound together. But the Jamaican didn't lose a stroke. Before abandoning the ruins of the bed, he folded my legs at the knees and had my cheek and chest up against the wall. I'd brought my hands back and over his head and they hung behind his neck. My other cheek was against his. Suddenly, he stopped the thrusts and held very still. He was panting heavily and must have been close to coming, but he apparently didn't want to do that yet. When his breathing had become regular again, he hauled me off the mattress, cupping one hand under my buttocks so that his cock would remain encased, and turned from the bed and swiveled my body around, facing his and my butt in his lap, while he sat in a straight chair.

He arched my torso back so that my head nearly touched the floor. My knees were bent on either side of his butt cheeks, and my calves ran back toward the front of the chair so that I could balance my body on the balls of my feet and maintain some sort of fulcrum leverage, as he grabbed my hips in this hands and slid my ass back and forth in deep strokes on his tool. He came in five separate massive floods of cum up into my intestines, and we both held position there, panting hard, until we cooled down.

Then he lifted my pelvis to his face, just as if he were drinking from a glass, took my engorged cock in his mouth, and sucked me off to my own ejaculation. Lowering my pelvis back to his lap, he pulled my torso up to his then, kissed me hard in the crook of my neck, and whispered to me that I was going to love our time together and so was he. I was close to tears, torn between pain and desire.

Then he let my body slide off his dick and into the wreckage on the floor. He rose from the chair and pulled on his pants, as those around us, who had been enjoying the performance immensely, pulled a pair of sweatpants over my legs and bound my ankles together. Then the Jamaican hefted me over his shoulder and hustled me out of the house to a waiting van with smoked windows, and we were off to the suburbs.

CHAPTER EIGHT: BACK IN THE COVEN AGAIN

I wasn't all that surprised to find that I was being taken back to Donatien's mansion in the suburbs. The Jamaican hustled me into the stone-vaulted chamber and over to the corner where I'd seen a young man hanging from a hook in the ceiling during my initiation ceremony. This time I was the one who was hanging from the hook with the leather straps around my wrists. The Jamaican untied my legs and stripped off my sweat pants so that once more I was naked.

I looked into the center of the room, and there was Doug, strung up where I had been fastened during my initiation to male sex. He had been beaten even more after they had taken him from our home and had been lashed as well. Blood dribbled from welts across his torso and legs, and I assumed that his back had been lashed too. But he stood there, glowering, defiant, not yielding to the coven.

As before, the room was full of studly men of all ripped body styles, dressed in their red leotards with uncovered crotches and butt cracks. The room was hushed, as Donatien stepped out of the smoke-enshrouded shadows. As before, he was naked except for the leather straps peeking out of the hair on his chest. But, upon reflection, I saw that he wasn't as naked as before. His cock now was encased in a thick leather-strapped sheath, with silver studs dotted around the leather. His smile was as devilish as ever.

Donatien strode up to in front of me and backhanded me from both sides across my face. My head snapped back, and I could feel blood in my mouth.

"You've been very naughty," he said to me with a malevolent smile. "Very inventive—and I admire you for that—but very naughty. Not only haven't you accepted my invitation to join the coven yet, but you also subverted one of my best men."

He leaned into me with his face, took my head between his hands, and gave me a deep kiss on the lips, making sure that he'd sucked my cut lip before he disengaged. I jerked my head out of his grasp and arched back from him. This brought our pelvises into contact. Donatien reached down with one hand and encased our cocks together. I felt rough leather and cold studs on the tender flesh of my dick. His other hand went to the small of my back, and a long, elegant finger pushed down between my exposed butt cheeks. His mouth went to my nipples, and it was impossible for my cock not to respond by engorging. He was

78

rubbing our cocks together and gently stroking them as one. His finger entered my ass and rotated around, causing me to gasp.

"Ah, I remember how sweet your body is," he whispered to my lovingly. "Thomas has reported that he took you many times earlier this evening, and that he found each position and fuck invigorating and highly pleasant. I feel you and he are going to be very good friends. So, tell me, are you melting at the prospect of being regularly serviced by our Thomas? Are you ready to accept the membership I've bestowed on you in the coven now?"

"No, never," I hissed at him. Donatien's teeth bit down on the aureole of one of my nipples, and I let out a little scream. He lifted his head and gave me a look of deep disappointment.

"Never say never, my friend," his whispered in a throaty voice. "At least don't say it in haste. Perhaps you should get some sense of what is at stake."

He then moved behind me, his torso closely touching my back. His cock came between my thighs, the head pushing at the root of my dick and my ball sac. The rough leather and studs gently rocked back and forth along my perineum. He took my head in both of his hands again and turned it to where I could see the trussed up Doug directly.

As I watched, the giant Jamaican, Thomas, reappeared in the room. From another corner, an equally giant, but thinner, Asian man appeared. Both were completely naked except for a sheath encasing their cocks. Light glinted off these apparatuses.

"Rhinestones," Donatien hissed in my ear. "Very pretty, but also can be very sharp. Luckily for our Doug, these aren't as sharp as they could be."

The two men circled Doug, like sharks. He gave them a defiant look.

"What . . .?" I started to ask.

"Shhhh," Donatien hissed at me. "You were quick to say no. Both for his own sin and for your flippant response to my repeated invitation, you'll see just how careful you need to be and how carefully you need to consider your words when it concerns the coven."

"No, please," I cried. "It's not Doug's fault. Not any of it. I tricked him."

"Regardless, he chose to stay with you."

Doug lurched in surprise, and his face showed a sudden grimace of pain, as Thomas approached him from the rear. The Jamaican had one hand on Doug's belly, and the other was hidden behind Doug's back, but I had little doubt that Thomas was positioning his massive cock at Doug's asshole. The Asian approached Doug from the front, and, upon a command from Thomas, the chains on Doug's wrists pulled his body up and those on his ankles pulled his legs up into the air. Both the Jamaican and the Asian had their pelvises under Doug now, their massive dicks poised to strike, and were arching their backs away from him.

Tears came to Doug's eyes, as the first inch of the two cocks entered his ass. Thus far, most of what had entered him was exposed dick helmet, and he'd been doubled before. Nevertheless, rhinestones must already be punishing the rim of his ass. He set his jaw, though, determined not to scream.

I screamed for him, however, as Donatien stood close behind me, his arms wrapped around me with one hand playing with a nipple and the other gently stroking my dick. I could still feel the roughness of his stud-covered cock running across my perineum, but I felt shame at Doug's and my respective predicaments.

"Give our Doug a little bit of the rhinestone razzle-dazzle," Donatien commanded in a booming voice. A bit more of the two cocks disappeared up Doug's ass, and now he involuntarily screamed. Rivulets of blood ran down his inner thigh.

"No!" I cried. "What do you want from me?"

"Tell me you accept the invitation to my coven," Donatien said in a hoarse voice.

"Yes, yes," I cried.

"Yes, what?" Donatien hissed.

"Yes, please let me in the coven," I said loud enough for all to hear. "Please, I accept your invitation."

"You realize that that would mean you could no longer have sex with Doug, don't you? Doug has forfeited his rights to be in the coven."

"Yes, yes, whatever you say," I answered. "Just let him go."

"But you want to tell me why you so easily give up a relationship with Doug, don't you?"

"What?" I moaned.

"You want to tell me that I give you a much better fuck than Doug does, don't you?"

"What? Oh, yes, yes."

"Yes, yes what? I want everyone here to hear it."

"You're a much better lover than Doug," I said. "You are and will always be the master." There it was then. Donatien was doing this out of personal jealousy—and out of a sense that Doug and I had tarnished his leadership position in the coven. I had little doubt about how serious this was to him under those circumstances.

"And so, what do you want me to do to you now?"

Silence.

Long, slender fingers went to my balls, and I could feel the pressure. Not pain yet, but the promise of pain.

"Fuck me! Fuck me now," I cried. "I can't wait for you to get inside me."

And then he was pushing into me from behind with an already-generous cock, further thickened now by leather straps and silver studs. He pulled my pelvis back, I arched my torso, and my eyes went to the floor, as Donatien's cock plowed up my ass. I had been stretched so much so recently by a bigger Thomas that I could accommodate the assault, but the studs did a real job on my prostate and ass walls. I grunted and moaned without reservation, which pleased Donatien greatly. I was reverifying his position in the coven with his adherents.

I looked up at the sound of repeated screams from the center of the room. More inches of the rhinestoned cocks had disappeared into Doug.

"Let them rip!" Donatien commanded.

"No-o-o," I wailed.

"Halt!" Donatien rescinded his earlier command.

"Doug's life for your total willingness," Donatien hissed into my ear. "My men must see that you truly want me."

"Yes, yes," I moaned back. "I'll do anything if you don't kill Doug."

"Untie this one," Donatien ordered, and my hands were immediately unbound. Donatien pulled out of me and came to stand in front of me.

"Kiss me. Kiss me passionately," Donatien whispered to me, and I did as he directed. He led me over to the low-slung altar, sat on the edge, and told me to make love to him. I started with another kiss on the lips and worked my way down his hairy torso with my tongue and licked the insides of his thighs and the helmet of his cock that protruded from the leather casing and sucked his balls. After a few minutes, he rose from the edge of the altar and had me sit in his place. We kissed some more and played with each other's nipples, abs, and bellies.

"Look like you are enjoying it," Donatien whispered. I spread my legs wide, arched my back, took his sheathed cock in my hands, and guided his cock back into my asshole. There was an intake of breath around the room at the demonstration of my submissiveness to the master. He pumped me for some time, eventually bringing my torso up to his lips and tonguing my nipples again. He guided my cheek to his; we were both facing Doug, still shallowly impaled on two rhinestone poles.

"Ruin him!" Donatien commanded the posed Jamaican and Asian. "Stretch him and cut him up so he will never be of use to anyone again. But don't finish him. Let him live."

"No, you promi—!" I screamed, but Donatien brutally took my mouth in his and stepped up the rhythm of his deep stud-encrusted fuck.

"Shut up!" he hissed in my ear when he took his lips off mine. "Protocol calls for death. You are saving him. I can still change the command."

"Show them you want it," Donatien whispered in my ear. "Change of position; you fuck yourself and show them you love it."

He pulled me off the altar, sat on the edge again, and I climbed into his lap, facing him, and descended on his cock. He pushed my torso toward the floor briefly to show to all that he was in to the root, and then, on his command, I rose up and down on his joy stick and rotated around it, until I felt him tense. With a powerful lift, he pulled me off him and into the air above him, and his cock shot off in a powerful arc that hit me in the belly. Then, he rose from the altar, laid me on its top, and sucked my cock until I came.

He stood above me, and his voice rang out. "Enough with the renegade. Take him and clean him up as best you can and then toss him out in the street." Then, as they released Doug and he slipped to the floor, Donatien turned back to me and said in a voice all in the room could hear, "I can't accept you as a regular member of the coven. But you belong to the coven now. When I call, you will come and do what you are told. You may have Doug back now; I have no use for him. But you will never again have sex with him. I doubt now that you will ever want to."

He started to walk away, and then, almost as an afterthought, turned and spoke again. "Have no fear that we will forget you. I'm sure that Thomas would not let me forget to call on your services often. And, oh, that reminds me. Thomas got his reward, but I almost forgot Shao-chuan. You must thank him for being so careful with Doug."

I was laying, exhausted, on my belly on the altar top. I looked over, in horror, as, with a big, evil grin, Donatien waved his hand between the Asian monster and me. The Asian grinned and walked toward me, his blood- and rhinestone-covered man meat still very much at attention.

For the briefest moment, I thought that Donatien was going to double-cross me and let the Asian tear up my insides too. But when he reached me, the Asian pulled off the rhinestone sheath and climbed up on the altar top, pulled me up onto my knees, and crouched behind and over me. He pushed my cheek down on the altar top with one beefy hand and swiftly entered my ass with a long, not particularly thick cock. But his cock was like a slithering snake, attacking my insides from all angles at once, playing a tattoo on my ass walls and prostate. He rose up onto the altar in a standing position, then, forcing me to come up on my forearms for support, and began pile-driving his tube down into me.

He was giving me long, deep strokes, and his hose was snaking around in my ass on the way in and out. Thomas had come to my front, now minus his sheath, and forced my mouth onto his cock. The gathered coven was getting quite a performance, and I had to restrain myself not to show that I was enjoying this plowing a thousand times better than what Donatien had done to me.

After only a few minutes, Thomas stopped face fucking me and the Asian let me come back down on my knees. He rolled his pelvis up on my butt and let his hose push up and down in me as well as in and out. While he was fucking me, the Asian's hands were flying all over my body, finding pleasure points I never knew I had. Thomas was up on the altar top now, The Asian's cock pushed down to the lower end of my ass canal, and I felt the Jamaican's cock entering me above the Asian's. I screamed and grunted something fierce for the room at large, but I was blessed with extraordinarily flexible ass walls and had been doubled before. I could bear this, knowing that Doug had suffered so much worse.

Their dicks were like pistons working on counterbalance, keeping me filled to the limit and rubbing against each other in ways that must have given them a great more pleasure than they'd been able to get in Doug's ass with the sheaths they had been wearing. At one inward stroke, I'd be stretched with Thomas's thick dick augmented by the Asian's flexible hose, and at the next stroke, the Asian's hose would go for depth, as the ass walls received a brief respite from Thomas's stretching.

Donatien appeared at my head, gave me a big grin, and kissed me deeply, as the two studs pumped away at me. Thomas gave a little cry, exclaimed in French, and bathed my insides and the Asian's dick in cum. With a noisy slurp, he slowly withdrew his tool and disappeared from the altar. The Asian, nearly as exhausted as I, pulled me over onto my side, with my butt spooned into his belly and side split me in much the same way that Doug loved doing. I almost cried at the realization that I might never be able to enjoy Doug at all in this way again, that this punishment had, indeed, ruined him for sex. The Asian was massaging my muscles all over the parts of my body that he could reach, paying particular attention to my pecs and dick.

I couldn't help myself. Before the Asian was finished, I was lost in his embrace, participating fully in the act. Being reduced to just one attacking cock came as a great relief. I was vigorously kissing him and enjoying the ginger taste of his mouth, when he pulled the helmet of his dick to the surface of my hole and spread his hot, burbling cum between my legs. He had managed to time our ejaculations almost simultaneously by coordinating the stroking of my cock with the timing of his own orgasm. I had almost forgotten that this same cock was tearing up the insides of my lover only a half hour earlier. Almost.

CHAPTER NINE: A RECOVERY OF SORTS; PLANS ABUILDING

The coven was good enough to dump Doug on the steps of an ER in a cross-town hospital and to drop me off at home with one of the younger men from the group with me to clean me up, straighten up the damage to our bedroom, and provide an alibi for me when the police arrived later that evening. After the police left, I went into the bathroom and ran a steaming bath. I stretched out in the tub and soaped myself, listening to classic music on a CD. I looked up and saw that the young coven member was standing, posed enticingly in the doorway to the bathroom, watching me sponge my tired torso, arms, and legs off, and apparently thoroughly enjoying the view.

He looked so young and fresh. He couldn't have been more than nineteen years old. A strawberry blond, with a smooth, chiseled chest. He was stripped to the waist and was wearing extremely low-rise faded jeans that showed a good inch of reddish pubic hair. His pecs were held high, and his arms were muscled, but not overly so, a very lithe youth. I wondered how his initiation into the coven had gone and how recently that had happened. He looked barely used.

"Okay, I'm settled back in now," I said. "Thanks for your help and for giving me an alibi. You can go now."

"Do you really want me to leave?" The young man asked. "I mean, with the alibi I left, shouldn't I be leaving some DNA around or something in case the police want to check out whether we really were together?"

"I rather think this bath will be taking care of that being an issue," I responded dryly.

"Oh. Well, it's just that Don told me there would be something in it for me if I came home with you and helped you get the place back into order and provided an alibi."

"Something in it for you? Like what?"

"You are quite a legend in the coven. All anyone can talk about is your initiation ceremony, and, well, I wasn't in the coven yet. But seeing you in action this evening—"

"So, the long and short of it is that you want to top me. Is that it?"

"Well . . . doesn't everyone?"

"Strip those pants off and let me see you. I'm pretty picky."

"What? Oh, yes, sir." And the jeans and briefs quickly came off. I nearly swallowed my tongue. Another long, beautiful cock, hard and curved up nicely.

"Oh, hell. Why not?" I responded with a weary sigh. "But make it quick. Come on into the tub."

The young man eagerly entered the tub with me just as "Bolero" was conveniently starting on my CD. I appreciated the clichéd moment—almost laughed out loud—and left the music running. None of this seemed real anyway. I spread my legs up onto the rim of the tub, and he slid under my buttocks, kneeling on his thighs. He entered me, his luscious dick curving up onto my prostrate, well before the rhythmic section of the music started to pick up its jungle-like beat, and he proved to be musically vigorous in being able to stay right on the beat with his long strokes, even as they intensified. Then we made more languid waves through the bathwater as he slow-fucked me through "Clair de Lune." And when he had bathed my insides with his young, hot cum, I graciously acknowledged that maybe he had a point about bolstering my alibi in this manner. He had spurted semen so deep inside me a mere tub bath wasn't going to erase the proof that he'd been having sex inside me this evening. I didn't bother to point out that I had the cum of four other men, including Doug, mingling inside me from this evening's exertions, which no doubt would really confuse a diagnostic lab.

During a particular wild Yanni number with even a more pronounced beat than "Bolero," I showed the young man that I could pound ass with the best of them as well, and he proved to be so tight, and yelled, grunted, and groaned so believingly, that I doubted that his initiation into the coven had been anywhere near as vigorous or stretching as mine had been. I was almost sorry to see him pull those jeans back over those plump orbs of his and slip out into the night.

In the subsequent weeks, the police only halfheartedly pursued the case of Doug's beating and brutal rape, being homophobic by nature and assuming that Doug had probably deserved all that had happened to him. I also later found out that someone in the office of the mayor was protecting Donatien's operation.

I had the bedroom completely redone while Doug was recovering from his surgery in the hospital. When he was returned to me, it took him months to recuperate to the point that he was even able to walk in the house. For weeks, he just gazed at me with empty eyes. And he only slowly became interested in anything remotely connected with sex, which was quite a contrast to the randy devil he'd been earlier.

"Did the doctors say that anything could be done about healing you internally—you know, good enough to enjoy sex again?" Donatien had said this wasn't going to be possible, but I held out hope.

"It would be extremely expensive," Doug answered. "And I just don't have that kind of money."

It was a week or more after my plowing by Thomas and company before I was able to walk around anything but bowlegged, as well. But I recovered remarkably quickly—and a good thing that I did, because almost from the beginning, I found myself summoned by Donatien at least once a week. I wasn't taken to the stone coven cavern again but was deposited in one of the lush upstairs bedrooms, where whatever coven member was receiving an award that evening would find me and ravish me. Often, I serviced more than one at a time. These sessions fed on my anger, not the least because I began to look forward to the sex that I couldn't be having with Doug.

More than a third of my sessions at the mansion were with Donatien himself. He would keep me all night, and an initial furious assault on my ass would quickly change to prolonged, gentle rocking in and out in a comfortable position. It was now that I learned that Donatien had a fetish; he liked to tie men up fully clothed and then slowly cut their clothing off as foreplay with a razor-sharp-edged knife, during which he'd get all hot and bothered and take his prey while they were naked, but still bound. With me, however, he was always especially careful not to cut flesh with the knife. I grew to suspect that he especially loved what I had to give, and that, no matter what cruel streak he had, he was protecting me from the worst that he could do.

I had discovered three very interesting facts about myself in these weeks. I had an asshole and canal that was remarkably pliable and able to retract back to reasonable size even after having been doubled by two gigantic cocks. And even more remarkable than that, I now realized that I loved the sex. I could feel pain until my canal had adjusted to whatever partner I was with, but it was becoming quite evident that I reveled in having a dick up my ass in all sorts of inventive positions and a cock in my mouth. If it was just the physical act of getting plowed, I would have enjoyed myself immensely. But I was being mentally and emotionally raped with each summoning to the mansion, and I could not come to grips with losing control over my body in this way.

The third thing I learned from this period, something that I would have gleaned sooner if I'd analyzed the events of the past several months, was that I realized that I was extraordinarily attractive to men. Even the straightest of men undressed me with their eyes and speculated about having sex with me.

I began to plot my revenge on Donatien, and, as I did before, I decided to use my attraction to other men to put this revenge into play.

I researched the members of all of the vice squads in the city's police precincts, and soon hit a bonanza. There was a thirty-something, ripped muscles, square-cut body and sandy crew-cut Marine drill sergeant type of a vice detective who worked out nearly every evening in one of the gyms I already had a membership to. He liked to work out when he came off shift, apparently to exercise off all of the frustrations and aggressiveness that came with his job. And thus he'd been given the keys to the gym to close up after himself after a workout that had extended into the early morning hours.

One evening, I timed my own workout for the end of the regular day. He arrived on the floor very close to closing, and I could tell that he was pent up with adrenaline from the intensity of his workout. I slipped into the locker room and made sure I was in the shower after everyone but the detective had left. Shortly thereafter the detective closed up the building after them, finished his routine, and slammed into the locker room, the workout not having come close to assuaging his energy and anger.

I was standing there under a stream of water, giving him a full frontal of my luscious body and soaping myself intimately, when he burst into the shower. He glowered at me from across the room, as I soaped up and stroked my cock, and I stared him down as his belligerent glare changed to a look of animalistic desire, and his cock started to stand to attention.

I turned off the water, padded back to the entrance of the shower room, and toweled off, slowly and caressingly, giving him both front and butt shots. I barely had my briefs and T-shirt on when I heard this animal howl from the entrance of the shower and he was upon me, still dripping wet. He threw me up against the bank of lockers, literally tore my T-shirt off my torso and wrapped a beefy arm entwined with ropy veins around my waist. He pulled my pelvis into his and I could feel the urgency of him— and he could feel my hardness as well—and he went for my chest and nipples with his mouth and tongue in loud slurping sounds.

I gasped and asked him to stop, which he took as a further turn on, which I had suspected he would. Pushing me down to my knees and taking my head in his hands, he commanded me to suck him, which I did, paying particular attention to pushing his uncut foreskin off his glans with my lips and rimming where the helmet met the bulk of the cock with my tongue and flicking his piss slit. I also moaned in feigned terror for him and acted like I wanted to disengage several times, which pleased him immensely. Tension was draining out of him to the point of him realizing this was exactly what he needed, but he was still tightly strung enough to take out his pent-up anger on my body.

He slammed his locker open behind me and pulled out several objects. Pushing me down on my back on the bench welded to the floor between the lockers, he handcuffed my wrists behind me and under the bench slat. He ripped off my briefs. Then he showed me a policeman's billy club, which he proceeded to lather up with salve from a tube. I babbled my fear to him and pleaded with him to stop and let me go. He just laughed and lathered up my asshole as well. He produced cording from somewhere and lashed my legs by the ankles to the handles in lockers on either side of the bench. My legs now were spread wide to him. Then he straddled the bench behind me, and started to work the billy club into my ass. I screamed and hollered virginally for him, but he was mightily surprised—and further turned on—when he discovered that I could take the billy club inside me. While he was rotating it around in me and pushing it ever deeper, he stroked my cock with his other hand and indulged in tasting it for himself.

He had only pushed the club in five inches or so when he was overcome with desire and exchanged the billy club for his own club, sliding in and out of me across the top of the bench. I changed my tune for him now, moaning and sighing and grunting and convincing him he was the best and that I was loving what he was doing to me. I told him I was dying to kiss him, and he released me from the handcuffs so that I could raise my torso to him and kiss him deeply on the mouth. He released my legs then too.

As soon as I was released, I pushed him away and made like I was going to make a run for it. With a loud, animalistic roar, though, he caught me and pushed me into the shower and up against the wall, with my cheek and belly flat against the wet surface. He turned the shower on full blast above us, commanded me to spread my legs, and, with one hand pushing my chest into the wall and the other on my belly pulling my pelvis back toward him, he roughly plunged into me and pumped away at me.

"I'm sorry, I'm sorry," he was moaning as he plowed me deep, becoming aware that he was (he thought) raping me, but not being able to help himself.

"Deeper, harder," I answered, increasingly putting my own butt into countermotion to his stroking. Eventually, he pulled out of me, his hot cum spewing up my back.

This copious and furious ejaculation drained the last of his anger and frustration from him, and he stood there close behind me, his dick still in me but withering away, as his breathing became more and more regular.

"I'm so sorry," he whispered in my ear. "I've never done anything like that before. I don't know what came over me. I just have all of this stuff built up inside me. I'll never touch you again. I don't know what to do or say beyond that."

"No apologies," I whispered back. "I loved it. It was just the way I like it. Please don't say you'll never do it again."

"Oh, God," he moaned. "You mean you'd let me take you like I was raping you again."

"Again and again and again," I answered, "Whenever you need release."

We kissed then, dried off, and went our separate ways after I gave the detective my business card with my home address and phone number on it.

He did call on me again, frequently, and each time we followed the pattern of his fetish, with him assaulting me in ambush, ripping my clothes off, plowing me first with a dildo or some other inanimate object, and then fucking me with his own tool until his cum and tension drained away; and with me going from pleading and resistance to acceptance and hot desire.

After several weeks, I felt I controlled him enough to tell him about Donatien's coven and suggesting that the vice squad should bust up that operation.

"I wish," he murmured to me as we lay, spent beside each other and he stroked my nipples through a ripped T-shirt and pushing the flash light off the bed the butt end of which he'd used to plow me before fucking me with his own dick. "We know about that operation, but someone in the mayor's office is protecting it. We haven't been able to make a move on it. I'd love to initiate that. It would make my career."

"But you'd move if the mayor's office OKed the raid?" I asked, my hand cuddling and lightly rolling his balls.

"Oh Gawd, oh Gawd," he whimpered under my touch. "Yes, certainly we'd take them down immediately." And all other conversation was then suspended, as he rolled over on top of me, grabbed my wrists in his strong hands and pushed them over my head, and entered my ass again roughly with his cock. He was wearing a cock ring with studs around it, and I moaned in appreciation as they did a friction dance on my asshole rim.

As much as he was pleasuring me, I was able even then to begin planning anew my vengeance against the coven.

CHAPTER TEN: REPLANNING AND ESCAPE

I was nothing if not persistent, so I went back to my research. This time I researched everyone in the mayor's office until I discovered that the mayor's deputy chief of staff was a member of Donatien's coven. All right, I thought, I'll just look for someone in that office who trumps his influence.

And it wasn't long before I did. I was just about to get into my car outside a gay bar one evening, when I noticed a big, black Cadillac parked down the street that I had remembered being there when I had arrived. The car had a low-number tag on it, which indicated it was an official car. I got in my car and watched for some time before a man emerged from the car and walked slowly, in hesitating steps, toward the gay bar. When he passed under a lamp post, I recognized the deputy mayor. His walk slowed, and when a noisily amorous couple approached and entered the bar, the deputy mayor changed his mind, retreated to his car, and motored off into the night.

I researched him thoroughly and planned our encounter for the shower at his golf club. Everything was set up. I displayed myself with a half hard-on in the cascading water, and he showed his interest, but in an instant my plan changed. I decided to play heavily to his obvious need. He was a bear of a man, shorter than average, stockily built, although not yet going beyond slightly padded to fat, and his body was very hairy. But his most distinctive feature was his cock, which, when he first entered the shower was hardly in evidence at all beyond an unusually large, bulbous rosy dick helmet. Although he was obviously aroused by me in the shower, his dick never increased in size beyond four inches. It seemed to be over two inches in diameter, however.

I decided that lack of length was at the root of his sexual tension and that if I relieved him of this burden, he would be putty in my hands. So, I left him there in the shower and cleared out of the locker room before he returned to it.

I did some architectural work for the city and thus was able to wrangle an appointment with the deputy mayor in his office one Saturday afternoon. I had indicated my schedule was so tight that this was the only time I could meet with him, and he assured me over the phone, having no idea we'd already met in intimate circumstances in the golf club shower, that he'd be alone in the office on Saturday but would be working that day.

I arrived at his office in a tight turtleneck sweater, making sure that the bulge of my nipples showed, and tight pants, making sure that the bulge of my basket showed off well, and carrying two foam containers of coffee, his laced with two of Doug's magic cock pills.

He recognized me immediately and presumably realized that I recognized him from the golf club shower room as well, so there was an unacknowledged sexual tension—and a wariness on his part—in the air from the start. He dutifully drank his coffee while we were looking over architectural drawings. He was sitting away from his desk in his desk chair, and I was perched on the edge of the desk in front of him, one leg planted in the carpet and the other one swinging gently between his spread legs, mimicking an intimate pumping action there and conveying in no uncertain terms that I was invading his space in sexual terms.

I watched as the capsules took their effect, him not realizing that his cock was rising far beyond its normal limits because of drugs rather than because of his unusual attraction to me and my obvious coming on to him. After a while, I decided to take him out of his misery, and, indicating the tenting of his pants, I said, "I can't notice but that you are aroused by me. Would you like me to take care of that for you?"

He blustered as I stood and stripped off my sweater and pants and gave him a good shot of me naked.

"We've met before," I said, "In the shower at the golf club. Remember this?" I waggled my cock before his eyes. "I had the feeling you wanted me there. Well, you can have me here if you like. Your cock seems to be interested."

He just sat there paralyzed, hovering on the threshold of giving into his long-resisted sexual desire for male-on-male sex and weighing what he had to gain against what he might lose. Only his eyes and cock betrayed his deep desire, but his failure to actively try to stop me was, in itself, a decision. I knelt before him and slowly pulled down his zipper. I freed his cock, which was a respectable six inches in length now, and he stared at it in fascination, as if he wondered where such a nice cock had come from. His fantasies were being realized. He was a full-blown stud now, and he thought that I alone was making him this hard, which, in fact, was technically true.

I pulled his pants and briefs off his legs and went to work on his tool with my mouth. He put his hands on my head, threw his own head back, and enjoyed his good fortune. My hands went to the buttons of his shirt, and I exposed his heaving chest and torso and ran my fingers through his chest hair. He was grunting and moaning in a way that indicated that he already was close to coming, so I pulled my mouth off his now-big cock, stood, and then straddled the arms of his chair with my legs, positioned my asshole on the bulbous head of his cock and descended onto him. I pulled his face to mine by his tie and deep kissed him until, on about only the eighth journey of his cock up and down my ass canal, he came in a big splattering of pent-up semen. His cock remained hard, however, thanks to the properties of the drug, so I pumped him for a few more minutes, his cum providing an adequate lubricant.

He sighed and moaned and told me how good it was and that he'd never imagined that it could be like this or that his cock could get as big as it did. He freely attributed the latter to my charms, and I didn't disabuse him of his belief.

He put his mouth at my ear, obviously not wanting anyone else to hear in this deserted building, and asked me if I could fuck him too—that it was his fantasy to be fucked by a beautiful stud like me.

I complied. I rose from the chair arms, brought him up as well and turned him to his desk. I pushed his torso down on top of piles of official papers and then crouched behind him and worked his hairy butt cheeks and asshole with my tongue and lips and stroked his still-engorged cock with a hand. He moaned and twitched for me. I entered him as gently as I could, and, although he winced in pain, he pleaded with me to continue splitting him. I pushed in as far as his prostate and rubbed that with my penis head until his cock produced precum, which I spread around his helmet with a finger.

He was relaxing now and begging me to take him fully. My cock slowly but smoothly glided in to where I could feel his pubic hair merging with mine at the root of my cock. I slowly and relentlessly pumped him deeply and shallowly, in turn, until he spurt another load through my fingers and down the drawer fronts of his desk. Then I finished him in swift deep strokes that had him huffing and puffing and yelling in ecstasy. After that I grabbed the tie and arched his back up to where I could reach his lips with mine and gave him a final, deep kiss.

Several "consultations" and half a bottle of Doug's magic capsules later and the deputy mayor was ready to put the force of his office behind a raid on Donatien's coven. I told my vice detective lover that the way had been cleared, and he went into action. Although I had been prepared to blackmail the two into doing my bidding, I was delighted that they were accommodating me on the strength of my attraction—and their individual needs—alone.

The detective gave me the date of the planned raid, and I bought a cabin in the mountains with considerable acreage, using inherited money, and moved Doug there, not wanting to be in town when Donatien's operation came down. I told the detective, and only the detective, the general location of where we'd gone and gave him my cell phone number so he could inform me when the deed was done. But I gave no one the specific location of where Doug and I would be. Two weeks after we had moved to the mountains, my cell phone rang, and the detective informed me that Donatien and most of his crew were behind bars.

I settled in to nursing Doug and trying to recover as much of his libido as I could.

CHAPTER ELEVEN: CAN CURIOSITY EVER BE STUFFED BACK IN THE CAN?

The fresh, clean air of the mountain country was good for Doug. Within a few weeks, I was able to harden his cock through, first sucking him off, and later, taking the lead in sitting in his lap with his dick up my ass canal. Merely days later, he was back to humping me in his favorite sidesplitting position. But the fire was not in our fuck sessions yet. We just hadn't reached anywhere near the intensity we had enjoyed before his ass had been reamed by that rhinestone-encrusted double fuck.

One afternoon I left him at the cabin and drove down into the little town in the foothills to buy groceries. I was hauling them to the car when I noticed a young, lean cowboy, decked out in a flannel shirt unbuttoned to half way down his chest, tight weathered jeans, leather cowboy boots, and a black cowboy hat. He was leaning against the bumper of a van with smoked windows and rubbing his basket while he watched me sling my sacks of groceries around. I smiled and tipped my cowboy hat, and he smiled and tipped his, and then I headed to the men's room at the side of the country store to take a piss before driving the winding road up the side of the mountain.

Unbeknownst to me, the young man followed close behind me into the small restroom and turned the lock on the door behind him. I heard the lock turn and twirled around to see that there were two of us in a rather small, smelly space.

"What, the fu—?" I started to say, not realizing I had turned him on so quickly or that he had been right behind me when I entered the john.

"Don't speak," he said in a hoarse voice, as he stopped my speech with his lips and pulled the tail of my shirt out of my pants and ran the fingers of both hands up my torso to my nipples. He was a lithe, handsome devil, with a deep tan and well-cut features, so I didn't give him much of a fight.

With little more preliminary action, he was undoing my belt buckle and pulling my pants off my hips. His mouth went to tracing my engorging dick through my briefs. He had me pushed back onto the toilet tank, where my butt was perched, and he was making appreciative clucking sounds at the back of his throat.

"Not here," I managed. "Anyone could be out there waiting and would see us both leaving together."

"My van," he answered. "I'll be waiting in my van."

He left me then, and I took care of the business that had brought me to the men's room to begin with, adjusted my clothes, and left the restroom, intending just to go back to my car and drive on up the mountain to the cabin. But, as had happened before, curiosity got the best of me, and I walked over to the open back door of the van instead.

He was waiting for me, just inside the van. He was naked except for his boots and cowboy hat, and his heavily tanned body was beautiful. He pulled me into the back of the van and tore off my clothes, as first his hands and then his mouth found my cock and balls. We were in the third seat back, where there was room in front of the seat from the access corridor for us to move. He had me in the seat and was kneeling in front of me, with his mouth on my cock and his arms running back along my thighs, hands cupping my butt cheeks from behind.

I let him suck me until desire got the best of me, and then I rose up around him, brought him up on his feet, and pushed his chest against the back of the seat I had just vacated. His hands grabbed for two straps hanging at the edge of the ceiling on either side of the inside of the van, and he dug his heels into the carpet of the entryway to the backseat, while my tongue and lips went to his asshole. He moaned and writhed under my ministrations.

When I went to enter him, though, I found that he was very tight and that he tensed up noticeably when the helmet of cock rubbed around at his opening.

"Have you ever done this before?" I asked.

"No, never. But don't mind that. I want to do it now."

"Never been fucked?" I asked again.

"No, never. I've always been top, but I want to be your bottom."

I had an idea. "I don't mind topping you, but I know where there's a truly magnificent cock that can be your first one. You can do me here, and then I'll lead you to where you can be fucked for the first time royally, and then I'll do you after that if you still want me. What do you say?" I suddenly had formed the idea that perhaps what Doug needed to get him truly started again was some variety, a virgin hole in a really nice stud. I remembered him telling me that he wanted variety. This could be my gift to him to try to make up for all of the trouble I'd gotten him into.

"So, what do you say?" I repeated.

"But I could do you now?" the young cowboy asked. "I've gotta get my rocks off soon, or I'll burst."

"Yes," I laughed, "Let's reverse and you go ahead and do me now."

I moved back, and the cowboy turned, took a seat cushion up from the second row of seats, and placed it on the seat we'd been straddling. This would elevate my butt to a more convenient level for his cock. I sat on the cushion and lifted my legs, wedging one foot in the frame of the open door and the other in the frame of the back window on the other side of the van.

The cowboy had a nice, hard piece, with a gentle crook in it that made it rise toward his belly, and he was quickly sending it up my ass canal and pumping with the vigor of youth. I stroked my cock while I enjoyed his pile driving. He came before I did, and so he nestled beside me and jacked me off the rest of the way.

When we were finished, I gave him directions to the cabin. He said he'd be along in a bit—that he still had to do a little gathering of provisions before he could go back up into the hills. He apologized for being so forward with me, but he said that there was something about me that had been irresistible and that also had told him I'd be willing, and he'd been up in the mountains all alone for weeks without a good fuck.

I drove back up to the cabin and told Doug, who was stretched out on the sofa, that I'd have a pleasant surprise for him after I put the groceries away.

A knock at the door introduced a surprise for more than Doug. I opened it, expecting to find my randy cowboy. And I did find my randy cowboy, but I found so much more. Standing behind him were Donatien; the Jamaican, Thomas; and the massive Asian. And behind them was my disloyal, lying vice detective lover. The latter was grinning at me, his eyes wild with tension and desire, and one hand slapping a rubber junior baseball bat against his calf.

From the shocked look on the cowboy's face, I could see that he hadn't been completely apprised of what Donatien and friends had in mind when they enlisted him to bring them to the cabin. I only had time to wonder if he had been signed up for this before we'd made love in his van or after before the Asian had come around Donatien and grabbed the cowboy by the back of his shirt, which was already being stripped from his body, as the Asian pushed him, face down, into the cushions of the living room sofa and began topping him to the tune of the cowboy's shocked cries of pain and dismay.

Donatien stood there, supervising, a big devilish grin on his face and his arms folded across his chest, as Thomas carried a screaming and wriggling, but sick and weak, Doug back toward the bedroom door and my drill sergeant detective pushed me over on my back on the dining room table, tore at my clothes, and got the end of the child's bat between my legs, pushing up between my thighs. I arched my back and screamed, simultaneously cursing myself for giving the cowboy directions to the cabin rather than quickly driving away, as, once again, I found myself sacrificed to my insatiable curiosity.

That's when, as my life continued to swirl down into the vortex, I knew this may never end.

CHAPTER TWELVE: RETREAT AND SAVED BY A MIKE

Donatien and his coven left us later that night after their debauchery, taking a semiconscious cowboy with them. But they didn't leave until Donatien had gotten a pledge from me that I would maintain contact and come to him whenever he called. I had been surprised that Donatien hadn't done worse; when I had gone against his wishes earlier, he had been swift and extremely brutal in his reaction. He told me now, however, that he thought he'd proven to me at last that I was not going to escape him—and I had to admit that he'd made his point. Now he just wanted to maintain a routine. Now he just wanted me—whenever he called.

They had set back Doug's recovery, mercifully not to the point of endangering his life, but, just when I thought we were about ready to fully resume our sex life, that once again was not in the cards for some time to come.

But my thoughts went more to Doug's safety now than to my own sexual needs. I maintained a cell phone I always kept with me where Donatien could reach me, but as soon as I was able, I moved Doug and myself down to a small beach house just up the strand from a public beach boardwalk and put the mountain cabin and acreage on the market. It sold quickly and at a good price, but I knew we didn't have nearly enough to get so far away from Donatien that he'd lose interest in toying with us. Not yet at least.

Life would have been OK at the beach house, if Doug hadn't gotten so frustrated that the only time I went out was when Donatien called. Doug said that just because he couldn't have sex yet or even go out in public, there was no reason that I shouldn't enjoy myself—that it was making him feel worse that I didn't get out and mingle.

So, I let him talk me into going out cruising one evening. I had no intention of ending up with anyone, but there was a men's bar on the boardwalk, by the name of Ricky's that I heard was a swinging place. So that's where I went one night.

The bar was pretty much what I had expected it to be. Guys playing pool, guys dancing with guys to a heavy-noise band, guys putting the moves on other guys in the shadowed booths along the wall inside a dense layer of cigarette smoke and an atmosphere of unleashed testosterone—all mighty good-looking guys, knowing the best place to ogle and be ogled and to get a little premium-guy action.

I decided to belly up to the bar and to do some watching and taking in the action and then, after a decent interval, going home and telling Doug that I'd had some of the action myself, when I hadn't. Anything to make him feel better about his slow recovery and its effect on me.

When I got to the bar and signaled for one of the bartenders to turn and take my drink order, I got a shock that sent chills right down to my boots, and I turned to escape from the room.

"No, wait, don't go," the bartender said in a pleading voice as he laid a hand on my forearm. "I didn't think I'd ever see you again, but I wanted to apologize for what happened and to try to make you believe that I had no idea what they were going to do. They waylaid me after you got out of my van and made me take them up to that cabin."

The bartender was the cowboy who had led Donatien and his cohorts to us. But I found it easy to believe that he'd been duped and hadn't had any choice in the matter, because he had been taken as brutally as either Doug or I were that day—and I'd been able to tell from his cries that, as he had claimed to me, he'd never been topped before that. If he had been one of Donatien's men, his first topping would be done in the subterranean stone vault at Donatien's estate in a satanic rejuvenation ritual, not up at my mountain cabin.

I turned back to the bar, signaled that I'd have the same brand of beer as the guy next to me was having, and gave the cowboy a smile.

"I know. I don't blame you," I said. "I saw what the Asian and the Jamaican did to you that day. I think I should be apologizing to you for getting you dragged into it."

"Thanks," he said, as he set my beer down in front of me. "My name is Mike, by the way. And I also hoped one day I'd get the opportunity to tell you what a hot lay you were that day in my van. Maybe someday again . . . ?"

"Could be," I was saying when someone down the bar signaled to Mike and he turned to get back to slinging drinks on a busy night.

"Nice taste in beer."

The voice, a smooth baritone, was coming from just beyond my right elbow. I turned and realized that it was the guy behind the brand of beer I'd signaled to Mike to pour me.

"Actually, it's the first time I've tasted this, what's it called, Samuel Adams's Utopias? Great taste, but pretty strong."

"And very expensive," the guy said. He had somewhat of a smirk on his face. He was very good looking in a beach blond sort of way, but he was dressed so nattily and held himself with such confidence that he screamed "entitled." And the smirk on his face promised spoiled bad boy as well. The two guys lurking behind him and oozing of "bodyguard" added to the image I was forming of him.

"Expensive?" I asked.

"Yes, it's about $100 a bottle. That's why I'm surprised you ordered it."

"A hundred bucks?" I blurted out. And I must have turned several shades of "I'm fucked" pale, because he laughed and his eyes developed a twinkle. I felt stupid—and a little resentful that he was having so much fun with my stupidity.

"No, problem, though," he said, flashing that big, knowing, superior smile of his. "I'll be happy to pay for yours. I heard the barkeep say you were a great lay. Play with me, and I'll pay for it. Hell, I'll buy you another one."

"Are you always this direct?" I asked, barely hiding my flash of anger. He was already getting on my nerves.

"Only when I see what I want. And I want only the best. You should be flattered."

"Well, I'm not." I answered. "And I'm not that easy either. Thanks for the offer; I'll manage."

"Sorry, my mistake," he responded. But he couldn't get rid of the smirk entirely. I decided it was frozen on his rich boy face. I couldn't tell if he was still playing me or if he just wasn't able to get close to genuine contrite. "I'll still pay for the beer, though," he said. "You didn't know what you were ordering, and it's because of what I was drinking that you ordered a Utopias. No reason not to savor it. Stick around and maybe I can take another run at getting you interested in a fuck. I'm good at it."

"I'm sure you are," I said, trying to show an edge of indifference without pissing him off altogether. If those two guys behind him really were his bodyguards, I didn't want any part of a fight tonight. "I think I'll just give a listen to the band and take in the sights for a few minutes, though."

I turned then, my back to the bar and my elbows leaning back on the surface. Right off I caught the eye of a magnificently built black guy at a table not too far away. We did a little bit of mutual assessment, and we both seemed to like what we saw. Another black guy came over to his table, though, and apparently urged the one I'd been eying out onto the dance floor. Before the black beauty left, he gave me that unmistakable "I'm interested; later" look. So, I decided not to run out quite yet.

When I turned back to the bar, my beer had been recharged, but the spoiled rich guy was now turned away from me and chatting up one of the bodyguard types.

I drank the beer half way down, in long swigs, taking a few minutes, but hungrily enticed by the rich, strong taste. A very strong taste.

I didn't remember much for a while after that.

I do remember leaving with the spoiled rich guy and the two bodyguard types, but I have no idea why I was doing so and don't remember having made a decision to go with them. The beer had an extremely heady effect on me, and I had little control over what I was doing—or any memory of agreeing to do it. It was all a hazy blur for a while.

I remember that the spoiled rich guy had a big, sleek, hunter-green Jaguar sedan. And I remember that the Jaguar had a big, cushy back seat. And I remember that I was suddenly naked and that one of the bodyguards was under me on the seat and holding me in a full Nelson and that the spoiled rich kid was half naked and was crouched above me and my legs were being wishboned and that he was fucking me hard and roughly. And I remember the glint of a knife, and the door to the back seat opening and a whole lot of yelling by a lot of people.

But the next thing I remember was waking up in sort of a lounge type room and Mike, the cowboy bartender, swabbing my forehead with a damp, cool cloth.

"Seeing better?" he was asking me. The voice seemed far away at first, but it got stronger and his handsome face, supporting a very concerned expression, was coming more into focus.

"What? Who?" I spluttered. I was laying on some sort of day bed, completely naked. It took me a moment to come to grips with being naked, and I wasn't fully able to reason it out.

Mike pushed me back down with a firm grip on my upper arms, though. He was sitting on the daybed beside me.

"Shush," he said. "Give it a moment or two. You'll come out of it soon enough, I'm sure. And be good as new."

"What . . . ?" I repeated dumbly.

"I saw him slip you that Mickey in your beer," Mike said. "I saw you leave with him and his goons, but it didn't fully register for several minutes. I was slinging drinks pretty rapidly. But then it hit me that I thought I saw him put something into your drink and I got a couple of guys together and we found him doing you in his car. I'm not sure what he planned after he was finished, but I'm sure it wouldn't have been pretty. Benji is known far and wide for making guys just disappear."

"But why then . . .?" I was beginning to come out of my drugged state, but I didn't have it all together yet.

"Benji's dad owns this town. He's the mayor and first citizen all rolled into one. And he owns the local law, too. The best we could do is pull you out of that car. That can't be taken any further. Not with Benji."

"But you saved my life," I said, pretty much fully lucid now. "You could have just let me go, but you came out and saved me."

I was overcome with the moment, and I reached up and brought his face down to mine and we kissed hungrily.

We made long, initially frantic and eventually languid love there on the daybed. He covered my face and torso with kisses, and I opened my legs to him and pulled him deep inside me, and we bucked and groaned and moaned, and he rode me hard like the cowboy he was.

I would not have to lie to Doug after all about having had a fully satisfying night on the town.

CHAPTER THIRTEEN: TUGGING AT THE LEASH

After multiple failed bids to slip out of the control of Donatien's coven and the pain of the fallout for having tried, it was tempting to just give up and give in and hope that Donatien would lose interest in toying with Doug and me. But opportunities were beginning tantalizingly to fall into place, and the curiosity that had gotten me into this mess was beginning to work its way on the possibility of both revenge and escape.

After Cowboy Mike's brave act of saving me from the clutches of the vengeful mayor's son, it no longer was safe for him to work at Ricky's or be seen much in the nearby town at all, so I felt honor-bound to invite him to live with Doug and me. And this turned out to be doubly advantageous. Mike proved to be a sensitive lover and companion to both Doug and me, and his ministrations to Doug worked wonders on my lover's recovery and regathering libido. Just as important, however, my mind had been mulling various schemes for revenge and a flash exit, but everything I could think of required help, and it would be a long time before Doug could take on this role. Mike, who had been roughly and dishonestly taken by Donatien's men was all too eager to help out.

I had already been working on bits and pieces of a loosely conceived plan. Doug and I both had passports already—and as soon as I had recruited Mike to a plan in principle, he applied for one as well. And I had been taking full advantage of the times Donatien had summoned me to his mansion for sex. Most often it was Donatien himself who wanted to fuck me—in his own quarters. I was only taken by anyone else as a reward bestowed by Donatien. I had used the opportunity of his brief absences from his bedroom to locate his wall safe, hidden, not too cleverly, behind a painting on the wall. More important, I overheard him telling someone that he changed the combination the first Saturday of every month. And another time, when he thought I was asleep but I wasn't, I was able to spy out where he kept the current combination, on a slip of paper in a paperback book in his nightstand drawer. I had even seen the safe open—and stuffed with money.

The other preparations I had made on the mansion end I had initiated myself. Donatien's fetish provided the opportunity for the first groundwork I laid. Because each time he took me in his rooms, he bound me fully clothed and cut the fabric away in foreplay before fucking me, bound to the bed, I brought a change of clothes with me each time in a duffel bag. After I had planned how to use this to my advantage, I started filling one of the compartments of the duffel bag with smelly gym clothes each time I was summoned, with the explanation that I stopped to work out on my way up into the hills above the city to Donatien's remote estate—that I had to pump myself up to give Donatien the service he enjoyed.

The first couple of times, Donatien's guards thoroughly checked the contents of all compartments of the bag, but they soon got lax with the one where I had stuffed the gym clothes and merely opened it each time and gazed at the dirty shorts and T and wet towel without digging to see if there was anything under them—which, of course, in this preparation stage, there wasn't.

And then, as my plan started to coalesce, I arranged a false police raid on the mansion during one of my sessions with Donatien so I could see which way he'd run. I had Mike call in a warning during one of the initiation ceremonies when I was being held upstairs in Donatien's rooms for his sport later in the evening. I wasn't sure it was going to work, because I knew that Donatien had the police in his pocket. But he wasn't taking any chances that night. He rushed into his room, decked out in his open-crotched satyr getup, and quickly changed and grabbed my wrist and pulled me behind the thick draperies at the windows next to a turreted alcove. To my delight, there was a door behind the drapes, leading to a spiral staircase that took us down to a tunnel leading into the side of a heavily foliaged gully just beyond the walls of the estate. There was a small garage just off the road there, where Donatien had a getaway car stashed. We were well away before he got a cell phone call that no police had shown up and that the deputy mayor had been contacted and assured them no raid was planned.

With this foundation, I went to work on a detailed plan. The sale of the mountain property had come through, and I bought an old, rusty tub of a yacht with an excellent engine and what looked, in the sales brochures, like a very nice two-bedroom bungalow overlooking the sea on the island of St. Thomas in the Caribbean. I berthed the boat up the coast at a small, on-its-last-legs marina, where Mike was able to find some part-time work and some free, useful lessons in boating from a beyond-the-prime boater who appreciated being fucked by a young stud.

And then I opened an account in a very private and cooperative bank in the Grand Caymans.

It wasn't only Donatien and company that I wanted revenge on now, though. The more I chewed on it, the more I wanted to hurt the mayor's son, Benji, as well for what he had done to me—and, even more important—what Mike had probably saved me from at Benji's hands.

Mike didn't like my plan much; he thought it was much too risky. I didn't tell Doug what I planned to do in detail at all, because I knew he would try to stop me. But the more I discussed it with Mike, the more he could see the elegance and "rightness" of the plan.

"But why include Benji?" Mike had asked. "I can see the part about the coven, but including Benji makes it a lot harder to pull off. Very risky. And I don't like the idea of you ever coming into contact with him ever again. He's unpredictable. And he's capable of anything. It's just not his sexual appetite and nastiness, it's the whole drug dealing aspect."

"That's exactly why he fits so well into the scheme," I said. "When you told me he was a high-volume drug dealer, the whole plan just fell into place. And it's also because he's the son of a powerful politician. It's just too perfect for what I need."

"But the cops are in Donatien's pocket—and Benji's for that matter, through his father. They just won't—"

"Which is why we'll go above their heads, why we need Benji for it to work well," I whispered to Mike, putting my fingers to his lips to still is objections.

I had been laying in the hammock on the sleeping porch overlooking the ocean, watching the sun set, naked and drifting off in the glow of a large slug of Yellowtail Shiraz when Mike had returned from the marina. He was crouched beside me, running his strong, sinewy hands over my body and bringing my cock to life as we went over my plan for the hundredth time, trying to be quiet in our discussion and foreplay so as not to disturb Doug, who was napping in our bed—his and mine—in the bedroom beyond.

"But I'm afraid. I'm so afraid for you in this. It's just so risky," Mike muttered.

"Shush, Mike," I said. "It will all work out; it will be fine. But for now, it's getting cold out here. I need heat, your heat. Make love to me. Please."

And then Mike turned me onto my stomach on the rope hammock, and he moved below the swinging sling. My cock was poking through the mesh and he crouched below me and took my cock in his mouth and held me there, swaying above him, doing wonders with his mouth on my cock until I was moaning for him. Then he came up around the side of the hammock and straddled it with his legs, as he lifted my legs up and out of the rope sling. His pelvis was between my spread legs, and I managed to dig the sole of one of my feet into the railing of the porch, and Mike held the other leg up and out as he worked his cock inside me, making me lurch and set the hammock into a counter motion to the stroking of his cock inside me.

We moaned and groaned in unison, as quietly as possible, but fully enjoying the working of our bodies.

Tomorrow. Tomorrow I would set the plan in motion, starting with Benji. But this evening, this sunset, this last calm before whatever came, I would spend draining my personal cowboy of his fear—and his cum.

CHAPTER FOURTEEN: FIRING OFF OF THE REVENGE PLAN

The next day it was time to put my plan into action. There were two difficult parts, and the needs of the plan dictated that I tackle the worst one first. Mike contacted a friend of his who was tending bar at Ricky's down in the town on the beach and asked him to give a heads up when Benji came into the bar. He was coming in every Friday night like clockwork, and it was now Friday. Mike got the call that Benji had arrived as usual, and I poured on a mesh muscle shirt and my tightest jeans and drove down to the bar. Mike wanted to come with me, but I told him it would spoil everything if either Benji or his bodyguards saw us together.

When I rolled into the parking lot, there was the hunter-green Jaguar. And there were the two bodyguards, leaning up against the luscious curves of the classic sedan and taking a smoking break. This was a break for me, as it meant Benji wasn't surrounded by muscle in the bar that might strike first before I had time to cozy up to him.

He was at the bar, nursing a bottle of his favorite Utopias beer and ogling the bartender, who was doing his best to ignore Benji. Benji was trouble, and that was understood far and wide.

I sidled up to the bar beside Benji, on his blind side, and mustered up the strength to get the plan in gear.

"A bottle of Utopias, if you please, barkeep," I sang out over the general hubbub in the bar, which was in full-testosterone swing. The band was taking a break, though, so the noise wasn't deadening. Benji had clearly overheard someone else ordering his hundred-dollar-a-bottle beer.

His head snapped around, and he took a defensive step backward. "What? Where'd you come from?"

"Hi, Benji, how ya' been? Haven't seen you around." I swallowed my fear and disgust and gave him a winning, innocent smile.

"Hey, look. My guys are just outside. They could be in here—"

"That's nice," I answered, trying to put a twinkle in my eye, "But it's you I want, big guy. You know you didn't have to slip a Mickey to me that last time. I liked your dick inside me, and I'd like you to do me again. If you gave me some space and we could do without the goons who were there the last time, I could show you a real good time."

I reached over and lightly mitted his package, letting my thumb run up and down on his now-rising cock through the fabric of his well-tailored trousers.

He looked at me suspiciously. But there was also desire and lust there, which I could tell were fighting hard for control. To seal the deal, I hooked my other hand around the nape of his neck and drew his mouth to mine and we kissed, holding it for a long time until I felt him completely give in to me. The Utopias tasted good—even on the bastard's lips.

When I pulled away, I could tell from the look in his eyes that he was gone to me.

"Half hour—after I've had time to enjoy my Utopias—under the Third Street pier. No bodyguards and no knives. Make me enjoy it with no strong-arm tactics, and we can make it a regular thing."

Benji was, of course, there, in the shadows of the underside of the pier, near where the sand met the water, all slathery and in heat. I was sure his bodyguards were lurking around somewhere just out of sight, but I thought I could pull this so that, over time, they'd let their guard down. I stripped quickly for him, and, although he had no helpmates and no knife, he still took me roughly. He pushed me up against the weathered, splintery wooden pillar, facing the shaft, and he roughly attacked my ass with his tongue and searching fingers until he was satisfied that I was comfortably open for him, with no concern whether it was comfortable for me.

Then he was fucking me hard, with long, cruel strokes, digging fingernails into my exposed buttocks with one hand, and pulling my head back in a painful position with fingers buried in my hair and with my back arched like a taut bow. When he climaxed, he had his teeth buried in my neck where it met my shoulders.

Everything he was doing was painful, and I writhed and let him know I was in pain—but with my eye ever on the goal of the plan, I used terms of ecstasy, egging him on, making him think this was exactly how I wanted to be taken. It was the way he wanted to fuck. He was mine if I could convince him we were well matched.

And my act worked. Over the next three weeks, we met often, and he took me brutally again and again. But he never went over the edge; I serviced him so well that he always wanted there to be a next time. I was sure that he increasingly was trusting me and that his goons were slowly losing their edge of attentiveness around me.

At the end of the third week, I moved to the next level. We were in the basement of his house, in his "special" room, and he had just fucked me while I was suspended in a sling and my arms and legs were bound to the four straps supporting the sling from the ceiling. He had been a big spender this time, investing a bottle of his precious Utopias beer as a sex toy to pump me with, mercifully neck first, letting the beer slosh inside me and to the floor, before he exchanged the glass bottle with his pounding dick.

"There, how'd you like that?" he asked when he was finished.

"God, you nearly split me apart with that bottle," I answered, breathlessly and my voice revealing the hurt, for which I didn't have to put on an act. "I almost thought I'd need a line of coke to manage that. It was great!"

"That could be arranged," Benji said with a laugh.

Bait set; line being run.

"Yeah, I'd heard you moved drugs, Benji," I replied. "Too bad it's small time. I have someone who wants a whole lot of the stuff. He's got a regular cokehead club goin' at a big estate up in the hills."

"Who told you I was small time?" Benji said. He was tweaking my nipples hard with a thumb and a forefinger, working himself up to fucking me again. "I can handle anyone's needs you can come up with."

Fish hooked; reeling him in.

"I'll see if I can hook you up. I think he's doing something special up there the end of next week. Could you get a large sample together by then?"

"No Sweat."

"Oh, god, oh, GOD, BENJI." He was cracking my nuts, fisting them and crushing them hard. I had to make him stop. "OH God, Benji. Fuck me! Fuck me now! I can't wait for it any longer, big guy! Stick your dick in me!"

CHAPTER FIFTEEN: EXPLOSION OF THE VORTEX

The target date at last had arrived. It was a Saturday, and it was the target date because it was a night scheduled for a coven initiation ceremony at Donatien's estate. And I was in charge of putting the virgin on the altar. Donatien had been after me for a couple of months to take up Doug's role—to cultivate and deliver virginal men to him for his coven initiation ceremonies, just as Doug had cultivated and delivered me into this hell on earth.

"You'll be a natural for it, stud," Donatien had told me. "Men flock to you like bees to a honey pot."

I, of course, had refused.

"You are not in a position to refuse," Donatien had countered. "Or I might be forced to put Doug back out on the street to do this."

There was no way I could do this—except that it fit in perfectly with my developing escape plan, so I eventually gave in. I didn't give in so easily and quickly that Donatien would become suspicious about it, though.

"Well, there is someone I think you might enjoy," I said one evening as Donatien was playing surgeon on my clothes before taking me in his huge canopied bed. "When do you need him?"

That had set the date for "operation escape." Today, Saturday.

As far as Benji knew, however, today was the day he was going to a big party up in the hills and setting up a big, ongoing score for his drugs.

Mike, Doug, and I spent the morning packing our old tub with what we couldn't do without in setting up a whole new life for ourselves.

I then met Benji at the town's pier late in the afternoon and we watched, together, his two bodyguards pushing off with a group of deep-sea fisherman in a charter yacht for an overnight cruise out to the offshore islands. This had been my hard-fought stipulation for hooking him up with the big buyer in the hills. I insisted that there be no muscle, no possibility of mistaken violence—and if his bodyguards weren't safely out of the picture—and if I didn't watch them leaving the scene—there would be no hookup. Benji took it hard, but he took it. The bodyguards tried to look stern, but they obviously were pleased by the unexpected holiday. And I had established over time that I was safe for Benji—at least that's what they thought.

Neither of the bodyguards was all that smart—nor was Benji for that matter. I had a chance to test one of the bodyguards two weeks earlier when he was fucking me by Benji's pool—as a favor granted to him by Benji. I had a small bag on the table by a chaise lounge, alongside the bodyguard's cell phone. I had been on my back on the chaise, with my legs spread out, and he'd been straddling the chaise below me and fucking up into me.

When it came time for him to change condoms for another go at me, I reached into my bag for a fresh one and, so he thought, accidentally pushed his cell phone onto the patio blocks and shattered it. I said I'd replace it for him, which was fine with him—he didn't care much; he was focused on fucking me again. What he didn't see was that I had switched his phone with a near-identical one in my bag before I dropped "my" phone on the stones and slipped "his" phone into my bag. I now had the device that would call in the cavalry.

So, on Saturday afternoon, with the bodyguards disposed of and Benji concentrating on his big drug score in the hills later, I suggested we stop for some barbecue and beer—Utopias, naturally—and hang out at his place until it was time to head for the hills.

He didn't see me slip the Mickey in his Utopias any better than I had seen him drug my beer the first time we had met. I don't think my drug was as potent as his had been, but it made Benji just a few seconds short of a reasoned response about anything. He noticed it, but he signaled that it was nerves. He wouldn't admit to being nervous, but I could tell he felt the effect, because he was on edge and even more brutal than usual when he pushed me down onto my belly and fucked me on the dining room table after we'd eaten there. I gave him the best performance of my life in wanting what he was giving me, all the time knowing this would be the last time and that I'd leave him with some satisfaction about what he was getting.

I was behind the wheel when we started up into the hills just before dark in the hunter-green Jaguar, but night had fully fallen when we reached the gates to Donatien's estate. This was much like the night I had first arrived there—when Doug had brought me here, as a virgin, to be sacrificed on Donatien's satanic altar.

The party scene in Donatien's bar room was also much the same as it had been on my initiation night. It turned Benji on—or at least did so as much as it could when he was half drugged. I had brought my gym bag, as usual, because Donatien had made it clear, as usual, that he would come to me upstairs after he was finished in the dungeon with the initiation ceremony. This time, however, I had more than fresh clothes and dirty gym shorts, T, and towel. Under those, this time, I had a small fortune in cocaine, thanks to Benji. These were the sample wares Benji was bringing to what he thought was a drug buy.

Benji had pretty much forgotten the drug buy part of the party, however. The three of us were sitting close together, Benji between Donatien and me, in a banquette in the shadows of the room, where the men of the cult, not yet dressed out as satyrs, were doing everything short of fucking on the dance floor and at the tables. Donatien was feeling Benji up, exploring his body, assessing the goods—just as he had done with me that first time. And he seemed pleased. And Benji, in his half-drugged state, seemed pretty pleased himself. Donatien was asking Benji the "are you virginal?" questions, and Benji probably didn't even hear them. I whispered in his ear what to respond, and he parroted what I told him to say. I didn't know how close to lying I was doing. I had no idea whether or not Benji had ever been plowed himself before.

Satisfied, the Jamaican and the vice detective who had betrayed me in my earlier bid for freedom showed up and carried Benji off to the sacrificial ritual in the dungeon, a ceremony that I remembered all too well. I was particularly pleased to see the detective. I hoped he was staying around for the ceremony part.

Although there was nothing noble in what I did next, I couldn't resist the urge to watch at least the first phase of Benji's undoing in the satanic ritual I had condemned him to. He had treated me so badly, that I could only give up my resentment and hatred at what I had endured by seeing him similarly undone. When the bar room had emptied out as the young, studly men rushed to change into their satyr costumes and join the festivities in the dungeon, I moved to a sort of musicians' gallery overlooking the stone vault dominated by the sacrificial altar and various apparatuses for serious bondage.

As I positioned myself in the gallery and peeked through the wooden latticework that hid me from view from below, I could see that the satyrs were already forming and warming up to the mood of the ritual by embracing and prodding and stroking each other, the cocks exposed by their open-crotched satyr costumes well on the rise.

Benji was naked, hung by his bound wrists from a hook suspended from the ceiling, and his curves and crevices were being worried by the Jamaican. The spoiled rich mayor's son who had bedeviled and delighted in bringing me pain had the good sense to be awake enough now to be screaming his indignation and fear. However, none of the hunky hulks below, other than the Jamaican, was paying him the least bit of attention. They were all well into working themselves up to a hot and heavy orgy.

But then Donatien, the magnificent leader of the coven, had arrived, and all had given way to him, gone silent, and gathered in a semicircle around him and the fettered Benji. Even Benji was quiet now, in awe of the moment and of Donatien's presence, and, most particularly, of the gigantic cock standing out proudly between Donatien's thighs.

The ceremony began. Donatien stepped up to the suspended Benji and the Jamaican stepped back. The semicircle of panting, entwined satyrs drew a step closer and a sigh went out over the tableau and lifted toward the vaulted ceiling and reverberated around the stone walls. Flashing through the sigh, a loud cry of shock and invasion shot to the ceiling. The cry turned to a gurgling long, drawn-out moan, reduced to a whimper. And then renewed cries of pain and helplessness.

I heard the voice of the master cutting through the cries. "Plowing!" Donatien bellowed. A cheer went up from the salivating crowd, and, as on signal, they broke away in groups of two and three, and the orgy of frenetic male-sex had begun in earnest. I could clearly see the writhing, moaning Benji now. Donatien was crouched behind him, his hands grasping the blond victim's hips, and was fucking up between Benji's plump butt cheeks in long thrusts of his monstrously thick and long cock in strokes that were lifting the pads of Benji's feet off the stone floor and setting the blond's body into a trembling, writhing dance of totally, deeply fucked rhythm.

I could clearly see that Benji was being taken as brutally as he had ever taken me. Satisfied, I turned and left the gallery.

I then went straight upstairs. When I got there, I knew I'd be alone for a good long time. Donatien and crew would be in the dungeon giving Benji—and each other—the planting and sowing and harvesting jazz for a couple of hours. I didn't particularly need to see Benji debauched as long and as hard as he would be, but I had no qualms about knowing it was happening. It hadn't been a necessary part of our escape plan, but it certainly gave me a nice sense of revenge for what he'd done to me.

The first thing I did was call Mike on my cell phone to let him know the ceremony had begun. Then I retrieved the combination from Donatien's night stand, opened the safe, and exchanged the packs of cocaine hidden under my dirty gym stuff for the stacks of money in the safe. I left the safe door yawning open, hard to miss by anyone coming into the room. There was so much money in the safe that I had to jettison my dirty laundry and fresh clothes as well. When counted later, it came to nearly two million in cash, in large bills. Some of it was in Euros, which I was much happier seeing than deflated greenbacks.

After dark had fallen, Mike and Doug had driven our old car that we were happy to be parting with to the shoulder of the dirt road running down the side of the estate's walls. Standing beside the open driver's door, Mike used the cell phone I'd stolen from Benji's bodyguard to call the nearest FBI office. Identifying himself as Benji's bodyguard, Mike said that Benji, the son of that important politician down on the coast, had been kidnapped and that he and the other bodyguard had followed the kidnappers up to a mountain estate. They were about to try to go in. And, oh yeah, the kidnappers had dropped some packets of coke from the getaway car when the bodyguards tried to prevent the kidnapping.

While Mike was talking, in hushed, panicked tones on the cell phone, Doug stuck his arm out of the passenger window of the car and fired off a couple of shots from the flare gun that had come with our yacht. Mike grunted in feigned pain, carefully laid the cell phone on the ground, circuit still open, and folded himself back into the front seat of the car. He then coasted up thirty feet or so to stop next to a gully, near to where I had shown him to stop.

While Mike was calling in the cavalry—the Feds, not the local police, and, with any luck, the Drug Enforcement Agency as well—I was making my way, the duffel bag full of money bouncing off my hip, through Donatien's secret escape passageway to beyond the estate walls.

I arrived at the car about the same time all hell broke loose at the front gate of the estate. We left Donatien to try to explain away the kidnapped official's son hanging naked from straps in his dungeon, thirty-odd men dressed as satyrs with their privates hanging out, and a stash of cocaine in the open safe in his bedroom and sped down out of the mountains and down the coast to our stocked boat.

Mike had learned enough from the horny old boatman to get us safely to the coast of Baja Mexico, where we found a bank quite willing, for a stiff fee, to cable transfer our new-found wealth to the bank in the Grand Caymans. Mike and Doug were both delighted with the cliff-top beach cottage I'd bought on St. Thomas, and Mike, Doug, and I remained there together and enjoyed our new-found wealth and peace and security ever after. I had located a perfectly good surgeon in St. Thomas who was laying low himself because of huge discrepancies that had been found in drugs ordered and drugs on hand in his New York practice and for less than I supposed would be needed, we managed to get Doug's insides redone to the point that he could enjoy bottoming as well as Mike and I did.

From then on out, whenever I felt I was getting curious about something, wondering if I'd enjoy doing something different or kinky, I gave a thought to the swirling vortex I somehow had miraculously escaped. Then I dug into my stash of Utopias beer and drank myself silly and nonfunctional.

ABOUT THE AUTHOR

Habu is one of the pen names of a former supersonic spy jet pilot, intelligence agent, male model, movie actor, and diplomat. A wild youth in South East Asia was spent enjoying whatever sexual opportunities came his way, and much of his gay male writing is about recalling incidents from those days and inventing ones he'd perhaps have liked to experience. He now leads a very quiet and ordinary happily married family life.

An American, he is a published mainstream novelist and short story writer under another name and in another dimension of his life. He has written or cowritten (with Sabb) over 500 published short stories and nearly 100 published erotica e-books, primarily of gay fiction but also memoir, straight fiction and ménage fiction. His hand and creative writing can be seen in stories and books by habu, sr71plt, Dirk Hessian, Shabbu, and Stephen Kessel—among unrevealed others that might surprise readers. The fictionalized GM memoir *Flying High, Diving Deep* is loosely based on his life experiences. He can be found at the adults only gay male site BarbarianSpy, which he shares with Sabb and Dirk Hessian.

Our authors always like to receive feedback, and appreciate it when readers post reviews at Goodreads, Amazon, and other sites.

Not all books listed below may currently be on release.
BOOKS BY DIRK HESSIAN
Xtreme Erotica
The King's Men
Shores of Tripoli
Prophecy of Noto
General Erotica
Constantinople
The Beautiful Way
Blue and Gray
Colonel's Treasure
Beginning of Time
Labyrinth
BOOKS BY HABU
Gay Erotica
Memoir Faction
Flying High, Diving Deep
Xtreme Erotica
Second Coming
Vortex: Sacrificed by Curiosity
Dark Angel Sounding
General Erotica
Habu's Christmas Balls

My Neighbour's Spa
Finding Amnad
Beyond the Beaded Curtain
Hard Knocks U
Man's Man
Trip Money
Clint Folsom Mysteries Compendium Volume 1
Clint Folsom Mysteries Compendium Volume 2
Grab Bag 1
Grab Bag 2
Grab Bag 3
The Indian Doctor
Sailorboy
Home to Fire Island
The Sporting Life
Platres Conclave
Fetish Galore!
Choke Hold
Literary Gay Erotica
Cairo Surrender
The Handyman
Homeward Bound
Journey to Mirage
Menage Erotica
13 Ways for Halloween
Luther
The Indian Prince
BOOKS BY SHABBU
Yap, Yap
Dirty Pool
Operation Black Jade
Cigars!
Angel in the Barn
Gayly Complicated
Despoiling David
The Tree of Idleness
I Met a Man
The Interview

Rough Road to Happiness
BOOKS BY SABB
The Legend of Holleystone Grange
Surprise Encounters
She is He
Wrong Man
Loyal to his King
Barbarian Tales - Book One - Traveler's Tales
Barbarian Tales - Book Two - Journeys Begin
Barbarian Tales - Book Three - The Inheritance
Barbarian Tales - Book Four - Road to Persepolis

~

~